LESBIAN BULLSHYT

A Novel By

Tanisha McMillan

 *OPAL BOOK PUBLISHING*

Copyright © 2009 by Tanisha McMillan

Editor: Angela C. Foster
Cover Design: Corinthia A. Kelley

ISBN 10: 0-9727011-4-1
ISBN 13: 978-0-9727011-4-3

Printed in the United States

Opal Book Publishing
www.obpublishing.com

Dedication

Thank you God...for making all of this possible. I know you gave me test so that I could have a testimony...

I want to dedicate this book first to my kids, Dominique and Moriah...for always believing in what mommy could do. You both are my inspiration.

I would also like to dedicate this book to my family and friends, who have always supported me and my dream, believing in things unseen, as though they were. Faith is a gift that I treasure from each and every one of you.

Lastly but not least, I want to dedicate this book to the woman whose heart beats in sync with mine...Darcie D'Andrea. You are my everything and everything is you! 3.16 FOREVER.

LESBIAN BULLSHYT

Prologue

I started this book as a way to vent about all that was wrong in my relationship and my life. In some ways, it was about being the woman scorned, but in other ways it was about self-healing and trying to understand my situation. Along the way, I began to see how many of these things were not unique to me as love does have a universal theme that transcends race, class, gender and sexual orientation. This is about my journey through all of the things that have happened to me, as well as other lesbian women, that fall under the category of bullshit. From many of the unspoken rules that straight women don't have to deal with or accept from even the sorriest man in their lives, rules which happen to be tendencies found in lesbian life, to the joys of finding true love, to the pain of failed relationships for whatever cause. I felt the need to write this while I was in the midst of what I learned to call "Lesbian Bullshit" and while taking the time to reflect on the path I had traveled. From relationships where there was the infamous "I love you, but I am not in love with you" excuse or that breakup where the one who wants out decides that they would love to be your friend because they still care for you. Excuse me? If we don't get along like that, why in the hell do you want to hang around me? Live with the consequences of your choice, your life without me in it. I could not bring myself to accept someone's consolation prize. She didn't want me for a lover, but sure, I'll tag along and hang with her, let her still enjoy the benefits of me without any commitment or without her having to do any work. BULLSHIT. If we did not work, we did not work. Go away and do your thing. Don't linger like a bad cold and please don't come in my face trying to work so hard at being my friend and telling me how wonderful I am, but when we were together romantically, that was an effort you could not muster. Damn, don't I sound like the woman scorned. Well guess what? I am. I have done the dirt and I have been the dirt. I wrote a book about it. Want to read it? Just turn the page.

LESBIAN
BULLSHYT

<u>Chapter One</u>

I want to get everyone's attention from page one, so I will start with a question that has been burning a hole in the back of my mind. Why do lesbians insist on being friends after a breakup? Is that some way of revolting against the system? My straight friends have never heard of such a thing and even if they decide to do it, it has to be under extreme circumstances. I know people with kids together, who hardly speak, yet here we are a lot of lesbians and the bulk of our friends consists of people we have slept with. Sounds like something on a popular soap opera. Like the sands through the hourglass, so are the days of Dyke Drama. Could you imagine? I would subscribe to the local cable channel that offers that show. Even the L Word couldn't compete with that. We women sure know how to dish out the dirt far better than our male counterparts. A friend of mine once told me that underneath those tits and nice ass is a man! Scary, isn't it? For me, coming from that straight world, I am having a tough time adjusting to what I have dubbed "Lesbian Bullshit," the stereotypes, life situations and relational drama that seems to comes along with being a lesbian woman.

"Well, you know, lesbians do have a tendency to remain friends after a breakup," says a friend of mine. What other tendencies do they have and why? Some tendencies need to be eradicated, like the tendency for lesbians to accept behavior simply because "that is what lesbians do." According to whom, may I ask? I tell you what, I am a lesbian last time I checked and I am not going for that. Wake up! If she can't commit, has emotional baggage or simply does not think you are worthy of time spent building a loving, long-lasting relationship and wants to downgrade you and grow a friendship, tell her to get a plant if she wants something to grow. The consequences of her choice are that she will not have the pleasure of knowing you on any level, at least not as quickly as she would like to segue into that friendship. How can we be okay with being the lover on Monday, best friend by Friday, and she's dating someone new on Sunday? Why don't we take our relationships serious? At first I thought it was a young lesbian thing, and they just didn't know any better.

As I have gone out and met other lesbians of different ages, races and places in life, it has become clear to me that we can never expect society as a whole to accept our relationships and take them as seriously as heterosexual ones when we are so quick to abandon those relationships without any work or true effort being put into them at all. We already know that society wants to see these relationships fail so there can be a huge "I told you so" and lectures on scripture and sermons about Adam and Eve. I may have had difficulty in my heterosexual relationship, but I never felt so much like Kleenex like I do now. For the first time, there is clarity and a true contrast of relationship expectations or lack thereof, lifestyle choices, compromises and commitment.

I honestly think I made a mistake. I thought I would get lucky my first time out and escape all the drama. I was so stuck in fantasyland of girl meets girl, girls fall in love, and girls live happily ever after. The only problem with that story is that it neglects to mention what happens when the girls have problems. No relationship will be free from stress and drama. Those things are a part of life. How we deal with that stress and drama is where the problem lies. I know I belong to the "Instant Gratification Generation." To hell with Generation X. Let me explain.

The generation I belong to, we know nothing of struggle or being denied anything. Everything we want and desire can instantly be fulfilled. We have cell phones, laptops, PDA's, express services, online everything at our fingertips. Extend this over to our personal lives and when something goes haywire, all we know to do is get rid of it and buy a new one. In two years, I have purchased 3 cell phones, simply because I did not like the features. I pay my bills online without leaving my home. I can even order pizza online. Now it's too bad I can't run my relationship like that, with convenience and ease of use built into it. Out of all the things in our lives nowadays, the only thing we have to work at would be our relationships, but because everything else is so automated, we don't have a clue. If it doesn't work, we throw it out and get another one.

Lesbian Bullshyt

Unfortunately, we are not talking about cell phones that don't work or computers that need to be upgraded; we are talking about people, their lives and feelings.

Perhaps it is because we have seen a growing amount of instability in the generations that came before us. People are not getting together and staying together like they used to do. In the media, we are inundated with images of people getting married and their lavish weddings and then a few months or years later, there is the big divorce. No one is hanging in there for the long haul anymore, so maybe that is making people in my generation just a bit skeptical on commitments and settling down. There are not very many positive examples of that whole situation working out, not even for the most loving couples. Even if it does work, it only seems to work for a minute. Look at Brad Pitt and Jennifer Anniston. Now I am not one to follow celebrity gossip, but I had heard that they were this super couple that was going to make it. When differences arose, they went their separate ways. I don't know about you, but I don't want differences like that and I want a partner who is strong enough to walk through the fire with me. Granted, some problems just cannot be overcome and that is a part of relationship life. However, if we were taking the time to truly get to know people, perhaps we would find out all we needed to know to determine that a long term commitment with that person would be a bad idea.

Before I came out, I had heard all of the stereotypical things about lesbians, U-Hauls and how quickly everyone seems to fall in love and move in together just to be moving out in three months. I never thought anything of it until I was wrapped up in it. It felt so right at the time until we stopped to think about it and actually talk. That is when the problems started and the demons began rearing their ugly heads.

We met in November, I told her I loved her in December and was living with her in January. We spent so much time together every day that with me living there just made sense. I had not been to my own apartment in so long that when I returned to get clothes, there was a layer of dust on everything. I had not slept home in a month. I don't think either one of us was prepared for what living together would do. I was prepared to live with her, but not prepared for her reaction to sharing so much space so fast.

We had different ideas and expectations of what living together would be like and to make matters worse, I took this single woman who had only been responsible for her dog and threw two active kids into the mix. Red flags went up everywhere, but we were both optimistic.

Needless to say, there were many uncomfortable moments and arguments about time and space and money. Most relationships that I have seen are based on equality and people talk about sharing things 50-

50. I have learned that sometimes 50-50 is not fair. Just because people equally share the resources does not mean that everyone gets what they need. I would prefer a relationship based on equity instead. Everyone should be able to get what he or she needs. I think having your needs met is a large part of a successful relationship, whether it be emotional, physical or financial. To me, it makes sense if one partner makes more money than the other that the partner who makes more carries more of the financial burden because an equal situation of 50-50 may not be easy on the partner who makes less. The same holds true for a partner with other obligations like, children and childcare. In an equitable situation, it may come out to 70-30 or maybe even 80-20. What sense does it make to have things equal if it means one person has to struggle to maintain that equality? That's just my opinion.

In the situation I experienced, what I did not have in dollars I gave in time. She was not the type to cook and clean and all that and it was a regular part of my life. She worked and I took care of the house, kids and dog. As long as each person contributes what they can and each person values the contributions that the other can make, why couldn't that work? I think it requires some understanding, communication and commitment.

Oh, I said the other nasty "C" word. Look out now! Just remember this, equal is not always fair.

<u>Chapter Two</u>

I can't sleep babe, I can't think babe
I can't live babe, without you in my life
Don't wanna go on babe, this is my song baby
I don't wanna do nothing if I...
-R. Kelly Can't Sleep

What started out as an erotic adventure turned into a tale about when love is meant to be, it finds a way. I wrote this story as an exercise in healing when I had to learn the painful lesson that in our gimme-gimme gotta have it culture sometimes loves is not enough to gain when there are a great many things to lose. I have been told that the first woman who shakes your heart is the hardest to get over. I never got to find out if that spark would have led to an eternal flame. Beware, love can and will grow from lust under the right conditions. The story is called *Whispers To God* and I am sure at least one of us have dreamt about the one that will make us whisper.

I stood in the doorway to our bedroom and I just watched you sleep. The candles that had illuminated our bodies as they danced together in love were still burning, and the light made you look like an angel. I loved to watch you sleep, standing here or you lying next to me, your breath slow and peaceful. I never thought I would have moments like this, watching you sleep after making love with you. Our beginnings were much more than humble and a moment like this was just a dream. I remember the first time I ever laid eyes on you…

"Excuse me…I can come back." You had your hands on your hips and your attitude was so stank.

"Hold up, wait a minute. Mom, I'll have to call you back." I got off the phone to speak with you, since you seemed to think your time was so precious. You were the doctor on call that night and I must have been your last patient. You had me so pissed off I didn't even notice how pretty you were. You admitted me to the hospital and I never saw you again, until months later. I had done some research on you, Dr. Naya Johnson. You caught my eye and I had to pay you a little visit.

"Dr. Johnson, hi. Keema McIntyre. After our meeting in the ER a few months back, I had to meet you, to see just who the person is behind those scrubs that made me get off the phone with my mamma."

"Oh really? Well come in my office, let's talk."

We sat chatting for nearly an hour and that is when I noticed you and those eyes. That's when you got me. There you were, all woman, soft yet rugged, sexy, sophisticated, nice honey complexion, short curly blonde hair and green eyes that were absolutely beautiful. At that moment, I knew I had to have you.

"So, Doc, maybe we can get together and have lunch sometime since our offices are practically next door."

"I'd like that. Tell you what, I'm going to be on vacation for the next two weeks, so why don't you just call me here after Thanksgiving and we'll do something."

"Sounds like a plan."

For some reason, you gave me a hug and the minute your body touched mine, I knew you had been thinking what I was thinking. The look on your face and the heat of your body gave you away.

After weeks of phone conversations and comparing day planners, we finally got together for lunch. We talked from the time we sat down until the time we got up. The more I talked to you, the more I wanted to talk to you. We had so much in common and we clicked so well. Our sentences overlapped and we were soon finishing each other's thoughts. I instantly fell in love with your smile and that wild fire in your eyes. You had the cutest accent. You were a Massachusetts girl so a beer was a beeyah, the only thing that separated us was age, but like Aaliyah said, that wasn't nothin' but a number. I could tell by the way that you kept reaching to hold my hand that age was simply a number to you too. You had just turned thirty-seven but did not look a day over twenty-five. Like your momma once told you, "If it's black, it don't crack," and she ain't never lied. You were beautiful. Me, I was barely 24 but I preferred to hang with the mature crowd. There was something about you. Aged to perfection like a fine wine and I surely wanted to taste you. This was new to me. I had only been out for about a year, but I knew that feeling. I could hear Usher running through my mind, "When you feel it in your body you found somebody who…" I had it bad and yes, you were the one.

"Earth to Keema! What's on your mind girl? I'm over here talking to you and you're in outer space somewhere."

"I'm sorry, I am a little preoccupied I guess. Let's get out of here and go do something wild."

"Such as?"

"C'mon. Let's go and I'll show you."

I paid the check and we left the restaurant. You had no idea where we were going but you were an adventurer, down for whatever. We rode in my car and I turned on the radio. Usher started to croon, "You got it, you got it bad…" You reached for the volume and turned it up.

"I love this song and I think that guy is so cute. Must be nice to have love like that."

All I could do was look at you and smile. We passed by a park and there were children playing in the snow. You begged me to stop and that's where we wound up, in the park playing like children. We ran, built a snowman, and threw snowballs at each other. We finished with snow angels and we sat on a bench enjoying the sudden quiet of the universe. The sun was setting and I looked at you, your nose was beet red and your eyes were watering, except it wasn't the cold that made your tears fall.

"Hey, what are the tears for?"

"This day, this moment has been so much fun and it is such a break away from my everyday life."

"And that brings you tears?"

"These are the things that I miss, the things that I long for, this is something my girlfriend would never do. She's so stiff sometimes and we've been together so long, it's just boring. Comfortable and boring."

Girlfriend? Oh God, please tell me she did not say girlfriend. I should have known someone like her; young, sexy, intelligent, witty, caring and so together would not be single. Someone was lucky, that's for sure, but what the hell was up with that comfortable and boring shit? That lucky someone wasn't doing something right.

"Naya, if it's boring, it can't be comfortable."

"I know. It hasn't been for the last year or so. I got so busy with work, I really didn't have time to care, to miss the little fun things that I used to do, like shopping on Saturday morning. She hates going to the mall with me. She hates my outgoing style. She is content to being quiet and to herself and she would like it if I just stood up under her all the time. I like to talk and laugh and meet people. We have grown to be such opposites. I didn't know what I was going to do, I had been feeling so trapped, but then I met you, this breath of fresh air, young, adventurous, outgoing. I feel so alive when I am with you and you have no inhibitions. You're such a free spirit and it was nothing to you to pull over and play in the snow with me. I want that in my relationship and I honestly crave it. I know she will never be that way."

"Breath of fresh air, huh? Well breathe me in," I offered, trying to lighten the mood.

"That is a tempting invitation, but it's been 10 years. She was with me when I wasn't anything, the residency, starting the practice. I sealed my fate when we bought that house and, well, you know how that goes. Too much mess."

"You love her?"

"Can we go? It's getting late and it's cold outside."

"Sure. I'll take you back to your car."

We left the park with that burning question hanging in the air. For whatever reason, you couldn't or wouldn't answer and I decided to not press the issue. I had learned from weeks of conversation with you that when you wanted to, you would open up. At your car it was somewhat awkward. I told you I wanted to see you again and if you needed to talk, to call me. I watched you get into your car and drive away. I went home to think. I laid in my bed staring at the ceiling replaying the day's events in my mind. I must have dozed off because I was startled when the phone rang. I never expected it to be you.

"Hello?

"Did I wake you?"

"No. Is everything okay?"

"I'm fine, but I have to see you."

"Okay, where do you want me to meet you?"

"I want to come to your place."

"My place?"

"Yeah. I just don't want to stay in this empty house anymore. She's working tonight and I don't want to be alone. We simply pass each other and I'm tired. I'm tired of living like this."

"Okay. Let me give you directions and I'll put on some coffee."

After I gave you directions and hung up, I jumped in the shower and made myself presentable. Never in a million years would I have expected that phone call and you to show up at my door with a duffel bag.

Lesbian Bullshyt

We sat up for a little while, talking about our lives and the situations we had been in. You were already a doctor and I was studying to be one. We worked out of the same hospital and frequented the same places. There was a lot of hurt in your relationship, but you stayed because it was safe in what can sometimes be an unsecure world. Couples like you were rare in the gay community, together for so long, happy and prospering. Inside, you were lonely and you wanted to be loved and to love someone, but not out of obligation. That feeling had long since drained from your relationship and it was now draining you. The two of you had met when you started your residency. At first life was good and the relationship grew, but then as you became more and more successful, the relationship grew strained. It was as if she resented the person you had become. Soon you stopped spending time together, and then you stopped talking. Then you both started working more. Your girlfriend would leave for work and instead of sitting alone like you had done so many nights in the past, you would now come talk with me. We spent almost every night together, sometimes going out, shopping, dining, just enjoying outside. Other times, we'd stay in, sipping coffee, talking, and laughing. I got to know you so well. I'd hold you while you cried as you mourned the relationship that you were losing, and then wipe away the tears with a promise for the situation to get better. Eventually, you had keys to my apartment; a huge part of my closet and you didn't have to call. I had gotten used to coming home and finding you curled up on the couch with a book and a mug of beer. I was the friend that understood you and listened.

I was the friend who had fallen in love with you, but I kept my feelings to myself. What started out as lust had grown into something much deeper.

We had wonderful chemistry, but I knew better than to approach you while you were in that situation. If I were to have you, I wanted your mind and your heart to be free. I also didn't want to lose our friendship. Except for a few accidental kisses, you kept our relationship platonic and I respected that. If that was a line you wanted to cross, you never let on.

Over the months, we grew together, sharing secrets, dreams, hopes, fears and fantasies. I told you about my ideal love, the one who would make me look up to God, close my eyes and whisper "thank-you". Our conversations were always deep like that. We shared so much and you were a major part of my life. Then you left.

We were supposed to have dinner that night, but you never showed. Although it had never happened before, I figured you got tied up with something at the hospital or maybe that night was a good night and your girlfriend was finally trying to mend the relationship. After months of you not being home and barely speaking, I thought she would have tried to do better and hold on to you, but she never did. After two days, I started to worry. It was not like you to not call or leave a message so I could know you were okay. I called your office and you were with a patient, so I left a message. At least I knew you were alive. I went about

15

my business, waiting for you to return my call, but you never did. Two days later, I saw you pulling out of the driveway of your office. You simply looked at me and kept driving. What was up with that? Against my better judgment, I called your house, something we agreed I would never do unless it was an emergency.

"Hello?"

"Hi, may I speak to…"

"Listen, don't you ever call here again, do you understand?"

"What?"

"Don't call here anymore!"

The phone clicked in my ear. I was in shock. That wasn't you, it was Tori, your girlfriend. How did she know who I was? We had never met, I had never called your house until today, we had never even seen each other. What was going on with you and why weren't you talking to me? I called your cell phone and I got the recorded message saying the number was no longer in service. I was freaking out, but there was nothing I could do.

The next day I received a phone call from Shayne, one of our mutual friends who also happened to work with you. She told me you never wanted to speak to me again and that was that. I was in chaos. Just as quickly as you had let me into your life, for whatever reason, you had just as quickly shut me out. It wasn't until then that I realized just how much I loved you. I went home to an empty apartment that night. When 9:00pm rolled around, I stared at the phone, hoping it would ring like it had so many other nights in the past, but it never did and as I lay in the bed, I kept waiting to hear your keys in the lock. Suddenly, all the feelings I had kept to myself manifest in everything I did.

Everywhere I went, something reminded me of you. In our small town, there wasn't any place I could go that we had not gone together. When I stopped to get coffee at the Starbucks, our usual waiter asked for you and I nearly broke down and cried. There were things in my apartment that belonged to you- your clothes, some books, jewelry, gifts I had given you, things you had given to me. As I lay in my bed, I could smell you in my pillows. I tossed and turned all night, missing you. As the days dragged on, I fell deeper into the darkness. My heart ached for you. I missed holding you, hearing your voice, your laugh. I missed the fire in your eyes. You were gone and I didn't know why. What had I done? It drove me crazy every time I tried to figure it out. Eventually I gave up. I buried myself in my work and my studies and tried to forget the pain I was feeling.

After a few months in virtual seclusion, my friends decided I had been down for too long and they got together to drag me out of the house for a break from the misery and a wild night out. When I came home, the light on my answering machine was blinking. There were three messages. I pushed the button.

"Trick, where yo' ass at??? Call me heifer and stop sulking around the house over that yellow bitch and get a grip girl. Call me Biotch!!"

My cousin was a trip. Always callin' somebody a trick. I'm gonna have to set her straight about that yellow bitch shit. Next message.

"Hi Keema, it's mom. I just wanted to check up on you, I haven't seen you in a few days and I know you weren't feeling too good the last time you were at the house. Derek misses you and he said you were supposed to take him to Toys R Us yesterday. Call me."

Shit! I was supposed to take my brother to the store. Derek was going to kill me. I had promised to not forget. Boy always wanted to buy some new hot wheels. I swear he better grow up and own a car dealership or something. This shit with Naya was getting serious. I could barely focus on work, my friends hardly ever saw me and now I was forgetting my family and my mom was noticing changes. Next message.

"If you're there, please pick up..."

Oh my God. That voice…Naya.

"Keema, I really need to talk to you. I know I have a lot to explain and I know that you're hurting right now…"

You know that I'm hurting? Woman, my life has been a wreck since you…whatever. I don't even know what to call that shit.

"Please call me. I really need to talk to you."

I just stared at the phone, thinking out loud. Six months and not a word! Six fucking months! She had Shayne tell me she never wanted to speak to me again. She could tell me her deepest secrets but she had to have someone else come to me to say she didn't want to speak to me anymore? Now she's calling my phone and she wants to talk. I was in love with her and I had never said a word because I didn't want to violate our friendship. For no apparent reason, she just up and left out of my life, broke my heart and never looked back. She had settled for the comfortable and boring she had come to me about in the first place. She was the one who violated. I was so pissed, but something in her voice got to me. I picked up the phone to dial the numbers. By the time she answered the phone, tears were streaming down my face and I was so hurt and angry couldn't utter a word.

"Hello? Hello? Keema, I know it's you. Hello?"

"Naya, why?"

"Keema, there is so much I want to say to you, so much I have to tell you. I know that I hurt you and believe me, I am so sorry. There is something I want you to see. Can you come to my house?"

"Your house? Are you crazy?"

"Keema, I am asking you to trust me. I promise, after tonight, you'll understand everything."

"Naya…"

"Kee Kee, please…"

That did it. Naya only called me Kee Kee when we were really close, usually in situations where we could have crossed the line, like the many times one of the massages she had asked me to give her led to what was supposed to be an accidental kiss. I wanted to be with Naya and my love for her was so strong at that moment, there was no way I could tell her no. No matter how much I hurt, I couldn't refuse her. I needed to see her.

"I'm on my way."

When I got to the house, there was a for sale sign in the yard that was covered with a "sold" marker. You came out to greet me. You were beautiful, more than I remembered. You looked tired, but peaceful.

Something about you was different. I got out of the car and I stood for a moment to look at you, drink you in with my eyes, and adjust to the sight of you.

"What's with the sign?"

"Aren't you going to say hello?"

"Please don't expect me to behave as if things are okay. The last six months of my life have been hell. You call me up out of the blue and you ask me to come to your house, the thing that supposedly tied you to someone you were no longer in love with."

"Keema, I am so sorry. Please, let's just go inside and talk."

"Inside? Where's Tori?"

"Gone. Now come inside."

You dragged me through the front door and into the living room. It was the first time I had actually been in that house and it was weird. It was a beautiful place, painstakingly decorated and cozy. I could feel the memories that must have been created in that home. There were boxes stacked in corners, some packed and marked, some half filled with packing tape and newspaper scattered everywhere.

"You're leaving?"

"Keema, I hope you can understand and forgive me. For the last six months, this was something I had to do. I had so much going on inside myself and it was so unfair what I did to you, dragging you into my life, staying at your house the way I was and…"

"Did I ever complain?"

"No, but let me finish. Keema, when I met you, Tori and I were going through so much shit. We were hardly speaking or seeing each other. We only came together to pay the mortgage and other house expenses. I was working more at the hospital instead of the office just to avoid going home. I was ready to leave, but when I decided it was time to go, her father got sick and I stayed when we found out he was dying. She honestly needed me and I couldn't leave her like that. I kept telling myself I would leave when it was all over, but there I was, still at the house four months after he had passed. Then one night I was working a double shift and I met you. I had seen you around with the rest of the incoming interns, but our paths had never crossed."

Suddenly, standing in your living room became unbearable when I happened to glanced around and saw a picture of you and Tori together.

"Naya, can we leave? I really can't be in here."

"Keema, Tori has not been here for the last two months."

"I don't care. If you want to finish this conversation, we have to get out of here."

"Fine. Lets go."

We got in my car and went back to my place. It was just as you remembered.

"Keema, I finally found my strength to get up and leave. I told Tori that I did not love her and I was not staying. I was tired of loving her out of obligation. Our life together was a cruel joke that I no longer found funny. We both deserved so much better than what we had been giving each other. The house is now sold and we're going our separate ways."

"That's great."

"Yeah, it is. I have spent the last few months healing and getting back to me."

"Why Naya? Why did you leave me like that?"

"I had to. I needed to make sure what I was feeling was not a rebound thing."

"Rebound thing?"

"Yeah. From the first time I ever saw you and when you showed up at my office, I knew there was something different about you. The more time I spent with you, the more I realized what a beautiful person you are. You opened your heart to me and gave me your time. You never asked for anything. I always felt so much when I was around you. I was free to be me without worrying about getting someone else upset. I fought like hell to keep it clean. I never wanted to cross that line."

"Naya, what are you talking about?"

"Keema, I backed away from you so that I could figure out if I had really fallen in love with you."

Wait. Did she just say that L word? Naya in love with me?

"I missed you so much and I wanted to be with you. It was killing me inside, but I wanted to be free to love you. I stayed away to get rid of my baggage. I had Shayne call you because I couldn't tell you this. There was no way I could look at you and deny my love and send you away. I knew if she said it, you would back away."

"Naya..."

"Let me finish. Keema, I know we're friends and I don't want to lose that by telling you this. The truth is, I love you. I did not leave Tori for you, but it was because of you that I couldn't stay. Spending time with you showed me what love could be like, not just in the beginning or some days, but everyday. You make me smile in my heart and when I am not with you, I miss you. I hear your voice in the breeze. Kee Kee, I woke up one morning and realized that I am in love with you and I don't want to spend another day of my life without you."

All I could do was stand there and listen. All that time we spent together, all the times I ever wanted to hold you and kiss you and tell you I loved you, I should have, because you loved me too.

"I love you too. I always have. The first time I held you in my arms I never wanted to let you go. I didn't say anything because I didn't want to ruin our friendship. You needed a friend and feelings complicate shit. You always acted so cool and you never let on that you wanted more."

"I wasn't sure about you, me, us, the age thing, my situation with Tori…the last thing I wanted to do was come at you like that and then hurt you. I wanted to be sure of myself, you know?"

"Naya, from the first time I laid eyes on you, listened to you speak, I loved you and I wanted to be with you."

"I wanted you too."

I could hear the lust in your voice. I had never really been aggressive, but at that moment, I wanted you. All of you. I had loved you silently for a year and now that my mind had spoken, my body had a few words to say.

I put my arms around you and I stared into your eyes as I kissed you for the first time and it wasn't an awkward "accident". Never in my wildest dreams did I think it was going to be like this. It felt like I was melting into you. Your lips were soft and full and I kissed you harder, with more passion. Our tongues played and explored each other. I sucked on your lips and a moan escaped your throat. I could feel you pressing yourself into me and I could tell that you needed me as much as I needed you.

"Kee Kee, make love to me."

I remember whispering a gentle "yes Naya" in your ear as I kissed my way down your neck. The scent of you was driving me crazy. I began unbuttoning your blouse and I unhooked your bra. I could feel the warmth as your breasts brushed up against mine. Your nipples stood out begging to be caressed. I reached down to feel them and they hardened in my fingertips. I massaged one and gently tugged at the other. I stopped to look at you and your eyes met mine. For the first time, I saw the fire in those green eyes and I knew it was blazing for me. You took my hand and led me to the bedroom.

"Kee Kee, I have wanted this for so long."
"Naya, I just want to feel you all over me."

I lay back on the bed and watched you undress. I walked up behind you and began kissing the back of your neck and licking my way down your spine. I could feel your body start to shudder. I reached my hands around you, gripping your thighs and I placed one hand over the essence of your desire. I could feel the heat as I slid a finger inside of you and gently over your clit.

"mmmm, Kee Kee."

"Naya I have wanted you for so long."

I continued to stroke you until your hips started moving with me. I turned you around so you were facing me and I looked up into your eyes as I kissed your navel, flicking my tongue out nice and slow, teasing you as I worked my way down. I kissed the outside of your thighs and I could feel your legs getting weak. You placed a hand on my shoulder to steady yourself. We quickly moved over to the bed and I threw the rest of my clothes on the floor. As I lay down, you followed me and the heat from your body radiated to mine. The moment our bodies touched it was as if we were fused together.

I leaned my head back into the pillow and closed my eyes as you nibbled my ear and kissed down my neck. You knew this was my spot, we had talked about it before. You made your way down my body, licking a hot trail of fire to my clit. I could feel your breath on me, the softness of your lips, then the fire of your tongue. I let out a moan and grabbed the sheets as your tongue danced around me. I tried my best, but I couldn't just lie there. There was so much I wanted to do to you, things I had only dreamed about. I rolled you over and began to suck on your breasts, one by one and I licked a trail down to that essence. I kissed the inside of your thighs and I could smell the scent of you. I playfully teased you with my tongue, then slid it inside, tasting you for the first time. I started sucking on your clit and I reached up to massage your breasts. You started rocking your hips against me and I slid my fingers inside of you. You started to moan and I could hear your breathing get heavy. I could feel the tension building in my own body.

"Kee Kee, you're going to make me cum…"
"No baby, not yet…"

I didn't want you to come, not yet anyway. I reached over into my nightstand and pulled out my strap. I watched you touch yourself as I got ready. I could feel my own clit starting to throb. You started to massage my inner thigh and you pulled me towards you. I positioned myself and slid inside of you. You had never been penetrated like this and I wanted to make sure I would be the first, last and only. My strokes were gentle and I could feel you get tense as you took all of me. Slowly we rocked together in unison, exploring the depths of each other. You began to quicken the pace and I followed your lead. You could smell the sex in the room and it was intoxicating.

"Naya…I want to feel you on top of me."

Before I could finish, you had me on my back and you slid yourself down onto my strap. I looked up at you, body glistening with sweat as you raised yourself up and down. I reached up to grab your breasts, and then I slid my hands down to your hips and rocked with you.

The sight of you above me was driving me wild. In one night, almost everything I had ever fantasized about was coming true. As if you were reading my mind, you leaned into me and whispered into my ear, "do it from the back". In one quick motion, you swung your leg over me and you were now facing away from me, legs spread. I knelt behind you and slid inside. Our bodies fit together like puzzle pieces. I reached around and cupped your breasts, then slid a hand down to your clit. With each stroke, my fingers slid back and forth over your clit, driving you to ecstasy. You leaned your head back into me and I started sucking on your neck. Your body started to shake and I knew you would cum soon. I began thrusting deeper and faster into you, holding you and sliding my fingers all over you. As your juices started running down my strap, you started to cum.

"Kee Kee, mmmm, oh shii…iittt…right therrreee!!!"

I quickened my pace into you and just as you were cumming again, I could feel my body start to shake and as I was slamming into you, my body went tense and all I could do was call out your name.

"oh shit…ummm….yeah…Naa…yaa!"

29

We collapsed into each other, sweaty, spent and tired. We had worked out a year's worth of desires and emotion. I held you in my arms and we cried together, and then kissed away each other's tears.

"I love you and I swear, now that you're in my arms, I am never going to let you go."

"I don't ever want you to let me go."

You fell asleep and I just watched you, peaceful and serene. We were finally together in a moment I never thought we would have. You were my ideal love and as I looked at you and leaned over to kiss you before I dozed off to sleep, I stopped to look up to God, closed my eyes and I whispered, "thank you". Thank you for bringing Naya into my life and for allowing us to finally be together.

We stay in places and situations for the material comfort. Now to me, that is absolute bullshit, and not just for the lesbians. There are two things that I think are the worst; Being with someone you don't love and not being with someone that you do. Life is too short to play games, live lies and be afraid. If she makes you whisper, hold onto her because that is a precious thing.

__Chapter Three__

Birds flying high, you know how I feel
Sun in the sky, you know how I feel
Breeze driftin' on by, you know how I feel
It's a new dawn, it's a new day, it's a new life
For me
And I'm feelin' good
-Nina Simone, Feeling Good

I walked around in a daze for months trying to deny what was in every cell of my body. There I was married to a man, but I loved her, yes HER. I had a marriage that should have never been. I procrastinated on the annulment, I had a newborn baby, and in the forefront of my mind was her. That experience for me as a lesbian was hard. Coming out when you never even realized you were in? Everything about life as I had known it was going to change. How could I explain all of this? I was perfectly straight until I looked into her eyes. She took me to places I had dreamed about, but been too afraid to remember. She was the reason why I could not sleep at night.

I don't think either one of us expected it. Hell, I know she didn't. It wasn't her place. She was someone I was never supposed to meet. Just in the right place at the right time, I guess. The look in her fiery green eyes is one I will never forget. That look changed my life. My thoughts of her made me shine on the inside and leap for joy. While waiting to see her, I felt as though I were waiting to go out on a date with the girl of my dreams. In the midst of all that, my home was falling apart. I was a newlywed with a newborn baby and responsibilities, and I could not see just how those responsibilities could fit in with this new found joy of mine. Life was supposed to be settling down into a nice comfortable routine. Instead, it was becoming chaotic day by day.

I wanted to be free to explore who I was and what I was feeling, not bound to a marriage and raising kids. The man who lay next to me had no idea of the internal hell I was suffering. He was my high school sweetheart. And just how exactly do you tell a man something like that? Especially when he worked so hard to get you to that point of trusting in him to actually have another child and become his wife? He had his moments but deep down he really was trying to be a stand up man, husband and father.

I now realize that for some men, it is much harder to maintain and hold things down on the domestic front. I didn't leave him because of my feelings for a woman. I left him because we had issues in our young marriage that I knew in my heart would only get worse. The person he was becoming was not a person I wanted to be associated with. My feelings for a woman only amplified the situation at home. With a woman, there seemed to be a promise of so much more instead of unfulfilled wishes and desires. Loving a woman came easier and felt more natural. It was something that I did not have to think about or convince myself of. The things that I spoke about to my husband, well, he used to tell me all the time that I wanted "that fairy tale shit on television." He really had me believing that people in love like I talked about only existed on television and certainly not in reality.

When I met HER, she spoke about the same things that I had desired. I was amazed. She would speak, my heart would race, and I couldn't think straight. I couldn't look her in the eye because I did not want her to see that my only thought was something like, "Where have you been all my life…"

I thought surely that if she and I were talking about the same fantasies and desires and connecting on that level, I wasn't the one who had a problem. I had come to realize that my husband and I did not share the same vision about the lives we wanted to live and the type of relationship we wanted to share. To me, he drank too much, he was a pothead and he behaved as though he was trying to be like Richard Pryor in The Mack, a '70s blaxploitation film. In my opinion, he did not have the skills to be a player or a womanizer. I was not the kind of woman who was just so content to have a man that I would just keep quiet and look the other way when it came to his indiscretions and fuck-ups.

Lesbian Bullshyt

I used to tell him often that gone are the days where women catered to their men and practically took care of them like their momma. Women like that are growing to be obsolete like the VCR. Don't get me wrong. Not all women want to be independent and free and that is okay. If you can be content with a man in that situation, more power to you. I just knew it was not for me.

As the days went by, I grew more and more turned off, partly because of my new feelings, but mostly because things were just changing between him and me.

He had begun hanging out with this one male friend of his and honestly, the way they hung out, I had to stop and think for a minute if at any moment both of us would be coming out of the closet. They were together morning, noon and night, passing up their respective women to be together. Years later, I hear the same thing holds true, even though he has a new woman. Same male friend though! I think Wendy "Diva" Williams says it best, How U Doin?

Not only did I not want him to touch me because I was disgusted with him and what he was doing, like lying, coupled with my suspicions of him cheating, and I was also hungering for the touch of another, a touch that he could never provide. When the baby fell asleep, I used to pray that he would not take advantage of that time and initiate sex. I wasn't so lucky. When he did approach, I felt as though I had to develop telekinetic powers with our new baby to get her to cry or do something so I would not have to satisfy that man's appetite for sex. I remember thinking to myself, "please cry, please cry...wake up and cry so I can escape." then off in the distance as if by a miracle, she would began to cry.

I was never so happy to get up to tend to a crying baby as I was at those moments. She had no idea what she was saving me from, just happy to see my face quickly appear at her crib. He knew something was different, but I don't think he knew what.

As my feelings grew stronger, I began to feel as though I was living a double life. A happily married woman and mother by day, and a budding lesbian my night. Who could I tell? Who would understand? I tried telling one of my close friends at work and was so nervous. She seriously asked me if I had murdered someone! Her comment made me laugh and it eased the tension. I was definitely glad that all I had done was come out of the closet and not bludgeon someone with a candlestick!

Things like this did not happen to married women, especially married black women. It is sometimes so much harder to be a lesbian in the Black community because of stereotypes, stigma and hatred that is bred within the church. Most black folk I know have heard many a sermon condemning gays and our "lifestyle". Being gay is not a lifestyle.

Lesbian Bullshyt

Affluence is a lifestyle. I have my moments where I am around a large group of black men and I feel as though I have done them some sort of disservice because I have found happiness with someone just like me and nothing like them.

Many of my brothers out there have looked at me and wanted to compare my feelings for a woman to their own. All they see is a sexual relationship, nothing that even resembles the relationship I do have. Being a lesbian is about more than "liking pussy" as one of my male acquaintances put it. It is about forming close, loving emotional bonds with another woman, building a life together, sharing life and all it has to offer. My sistahs have often turned up their noses wondering how I could forgo dick for a woman. Most people hear the word "gay" and all they can think of is sex, as if every relationship is solely based on all that is physical. I think any straight person would take offense at having their relationship reduced to what goes on in their bedroom. I still love my men Morris Chestnut (That is my husband right there. He was HOT in The Best Man), The Rock (Yes, I can smell what you cookin' with your fine ass) and Brad Pitt (SEXY white boy, although I did not pay him any mind until Troy.) The only difference between the straight women and me is that although I like these guys, I have no desire to sleep with them. I think Morris is a sexy black man. I love the personality of The Rock and he has a very nice body and I think the same of Brad. Do I want to jump their bones? No.

I was scared out of my mind not understanding how my life would change with these new feelings. I would lie in my bed at night, stare at the ceiling and cry in the dark as I racked my brain trying to figure out a way that I could live my life without changing it. Could I stay married to that man and forget about how I felt? Could I overlook that curiosity? Could I leave and just not be with anyone, ever? I knew that I could not and that was what fueled my tears. There was no escape from the truth. I was past curious. Even though no intimate moments had been shared, there would be no going back. My thoughts about loving a woman and being intimate with her came to me as naturally as my breathing. It required no work, no thought, and no extra energy. It was just who I was.

Being with guys always required work. I can remember being in high school with some of my girl friends and they would be going crazy over the next new male pop star and when it came down to it, I did not share their enthusiasm. Sure, the guy could have been cute, but whoever he was did not excite me the way they he did my friends. Honestly, the only pop icon that I have ever been crazy over is Janet Jackson. I guess I should have known back then. Ms. Jackson has always caught my eye in a way that no boy or a man ever did.

The only guy I was really attracted to in high school was someone who I thought was brilliant. I watched him leap for joy at acing an AP chemistry test. That brilliance made him sexy and that turned me on. He was cute too. Outside of that, I always felt awkward around boys and uneasy about what they thought of me and what they wanted from me.

My first boyfriend cheated on me because I did not "put out enough," as he put it. He was a few years older than me and I chalked up my unwillingness to engage in sex as just me not being mentally ready. Honestly, it just didn't do anything for me. It never occurred to me that maybe I was unwilling because I just did not have sexual feelings for him.

When I got older, I had a fascination with sex, maybe because I wanted to find a way to make it excite me like it did everyone else. Outside of that, it did not represent something deeply emotional and connecting. I always felt empty and unfulfilled afterwards, even if I had experienced an orgasm. It was always like, "is that it?" or "why did we do this again?"

The man I married won me with his friendly nature. He was not so aggressive about sex. He was my friend. That was what made him different. He did not pressure me about sex. His laid back approach was one I could handle as a teenager, and I could be the initiator when I wanted the experience and the let down. Even as a married woman, sex was like a big let down. I knew I loved him as much as I could, but that connection just was not there. At first, I thought we weren't doing it right or not enough, but no matter how much we did it or all the different ways, it was always the same. Eventually I began to accept the fact that sex must just be that way. I had nothing to compare it to, so what else was I to think? Looking back, I now know that the love was different than what I experience now. I loved him because that was what I was supposed to do. He was a guy, I was a girl, he was cute, we had a baby together. I took the path that I was expected to, the path that was familiar.

As a teenager, I could not understand what all the fuss was about, but I learned to talk about boys a lot because that is what girls my age did. I needed to divert attention away from the way I stared at some of the girls in my class and be careful about how I expressed just how pretty I thought they were. I cared for a few of them and it did bother me when I had to watch them go through the drama with their various boyfriends. I knew that if given the chance, I could do a much better job. Those were my thoughts, but I didn't have a word for how I felt. I used to think that it was just a normal girl thing to care for your close female friends. But it never occurred to me that if that was the case, how come I did not have that feeling about all of them? I can't remember knowing about lesbianism as a child or even as a teenager. I had heard about it briefly in Latin class when we talked about the island of Lesbos, where all the women hung out. Other than that, I honestly don't think I knew about lesbianism until a woman with beautiful green eyes stared straight into my soul.

There were girls I liked, but there never was a connection between that liking and sexual desire. When this woman looked at me it was as though she was staring right through me to the core of my being, seeing me for the person I did not yet know I was. I remember the discomfort I felt sitting in that chair in her office while she appeared calm and at ease with herself. She hugged me and it felt like I had been shocked all over my body. It was weird. I knew something had changed, but I didn't know what.

Soon after that encounter, the dreams began. I would wake up with pounding headaches as I recalled the risqué material from my slumber. Those were my first erotic dreams and they were so vivid. I felt so peaceful, so aroused and it all just felt …good. I wanted her, we were together, making love and the feelings and sensations were new and strong and they felt right. When I awoke to reality, it was all a mess of confusion. How could I make my dreams a reality? Should they even become reality? I tried to fight that feeling, bury it, push it away and whenever I felt it, I would make sure that I had passionate sex that night with my husband. I needed to do something to make it go away, but no matter how aggressive I was, no matter how many times, the feeling still remained and now I had this burning question in my mind. "What would it be like with her?" I thought about her at work, before I drifted off to sleep and when I woke up in the morning. I wanted to know what it was like to kiss her, to hold her, to stare into her eyes, and for once not have that empty feeling. I wanted to experience what I had dreamt about night after night.

I never did have a chance with the woman with the green eyes. She had already captured the heart of someone and I may have rocked the boat a little bit with what I felt for her. It all happened so fast and I was unprepared and I didn't know how to act. If ever she turns the pages of this book and realizes it was her, those eyes, her zest for life, her strut, and that cute Massachusetts accent that set my soul on fire, I want her to know that she changed my life for the better in more ways than one.

I understand and now know comfortable and boring and its place in a solid relationship. I'll bet you still don't look a day over 25 and for whatever drama I caused back then, I am sorry. I do hope that one day our paths will cross again and we can have coffee and stroll through a bookstore like old friends.

At the time that I was going through all of this, I never had time to think about what my husband was going through. We had begun living in shifts in the house, me gone all day at work and him at home with the kids, then me home at night and him out in the streets. I spent my evenings in, surfing the Internet or hanging out with my closest friend who knew what was going on in my life. I know it is easy for anyone to say that I left him because of my changing sexuality but that wasn't it. No one wants to disrupt his or her life in such a way and believe me I was no different. There were other problems in the marriage that just made it harder to stay, no matter what I was going through. With that aside, I now wonder how hard it was for him to lose his wife, his marriage, his life. We had been together for six years, had two beautiful children and memories together. We struggled and laughed together, and worked hard to maintain a relationship the adults around us thought was doomed. We beat the statistical odds as teenage parents. We were together when our child entered kindergarten. There were no statistics that could have predicted how our relationship ended.

I tried to be honest, telling him about my feelings but I don't think he knew how serious it was. I was in college at the time and I remember him telling me to go off and explore my feelings because "that is what college girls do," mess around with other girls. I do have to give him some sort of credit for trying to be supportive. The only problem is that he underestimated how I felt and what it was all about. I was more than an inexperienced college girl. I was a wife and a mother. I knew about emotional needs and fulfillment. It was about more than getting a little freaky and being a "college girl gone wild". I did what he told me to and I met a nice girl and we started talking on the phone and eventually hanging out and it got to the point where I was talking to her at work, at home and seeing her when I could. She was the first woman I ever kissed and the first woman to do anything to me sexually. All those years of feeling unfulfilled vanished in the dark of night as we explored each other. I remember breathing a sigh of relief, as if to say, "Finally, I have found it."

My life could never go back to what it was after that night. I knew that I could not ever be with a man again and suffer that emptiness. I cried the last time my husband tried to make love to me. He felt that he could satisfy my desires by basing more of our sexual experience on oral sex, as if the feeling of having my pussy licked would be enough to satisfy me. He figured he would only focus on the sexual aspect of being lesbian.

What I felt was about more than a sexual encounter. I did not want to be identified as a heterosexual woman with a husband. I wanted the same life I had, just with a woman. My heart and my mind were no longer there with him and it was destroying my soul. Everything had changed. I felt so comfortable with the thought of having a partner, a same-sex spouse as opposed to being his wife. I felt better about not liking to wear dresses and being such a tomboy. There was so much validation in my coming to terms with my sexuality. Suddenly everything made sense.

With fear and sadness, I sent him on his way. A few times he tried to come back and work things out, but there would be no return. I couldn't be his wife, his lover or even his friend. We had hurt each other many more times than I care to remember and we had said and done things that could never be erased. He represented many things in my life that I wanted to forget. After a while, he seemed to accept his loss and he stopped coming around. For that, I was glad and I continued on my journey of self-discovery. I never heard about his hurt until years later when he had found happiness again. For his pain as a person, as a man losing his wife and his family as he knew it, I am sorry. If I had known what the road held, I would have walked the path alone. While he works still at being a better man, father and husband, I am working on establishing my life and strengthening the relationships that I hold dear. I wish him well on his journey.

My children were fairly young when I came out. My eldest, Dominique, was five and my youngest, Moriah, was barely a year old. As the time passes I am seeing how my coming out is impacting their lives. So far so good, although I must admit in the beginning it was harder for Dominique because she had memories of her father and I together and being a family. Had he been a more stand up man, the transition may not have been so difficult. When I divorced him, he divorced our kids and that was not fair and remains something I will never forgive him for. No matter whatever happened between he and I, my love for our children and my dedication to them has never wavered.

When the first woman came into my life, I'll admit, in the beginning, she was for entertainment purposes only. She was not to meet my kids, my family, nobody. She was someone to creep around with in the darkness of night. I had to be careful about who I was letting into my life. I did not want the kids to meet all kinds of different people with no sense of consistency. It was no different than dating a new man. I had my rules.

After some time, I felt that some rules should be broken and I wound up introducing them to the woman who has grown to be like a second mother to them. I'll admit, it was different to hear Moriah call someone else "mommy", but it was more of a testament to how much we had all grown together as a family. When a child comes to you seeking comfort when they are sick and will fall asleep in your arms, there is definitely some bonding going on. I thought it was the most natural, most beautiful thing to watch my child sleeping peacefully on the chest of this woman who she had grown to love as her mommy.

Chapter Four

I am in love with you
You set me free
I can't do this thing called life without you here with me cause I'm
Dangerously in love with you
I'll never leave
Just keep lovin' me the way I love you lovin' me
-Beyonce, Dangerously In Love

Why is it that mothers always have to act foolish about girlfriends? Now this is not to say that they all behave that way, this is just about mine. This is the chapter of LBS to make you laugh and shake your head at perhaps what may be fond memories of your own mother and her inability and/or unwillingness to deal with your life and identity. Be careful moms, there are some things you do not want to say to your lesbian daughter, even if she is making mistakes in her relationship.

"You follow her around like she is something good to eat."

In the midst of a heated argument, my mother let that slip out of her mouth. I don't think she knew where my brain went at that moment. How on earth could I possibly respond to her statement without being rude or enlightening her on one of the many joys of lesbian sex? All I could

46

think was "Momma, if you knew like I did, you would understand. Did you not see us downing all that pineapple juice the other night? She tastes smooth and creamy and just plain good!" I wanted to tell her that the woman in question had a taste that was out of this world, better than my Starbucks coffee and even a milkshake from McDonald's. To know that flavor was to know ecstasy.

I had hoped that I would bring someone home that my family would like, accept and grow to love. That is still my hope. I wanted my family to see that this relationship was no different than any other in the sense that there were two people who loved each other and were trying to build a life together. Never mind that we were both women. From that relationship, my kids were surrounded in a home with love and equality and I think they will turn out to be better people because of it. They got to see what love really looks like. This is not to say that the true face of love does not exist in heterosexual relationships, it is just more of what has always been.

Same-sex relationships offer different dynamics and they challenge societal roles about gender. There were no gender-designated chores because everyone was an equal. That equality tends to be missing sometimes in heterosexual relationships because of stronger power dynamics that exist outside the home. Amidst all of the bullshit, let us not forget that even the most skilled woman only makes seventy five cents to a man's dollar.

I look at the woman in my life and there are certain things that stand out about the person she is. She gets up in the morning to go to work and I roll over in bed to her spot and snooze peacefully in her scent on the pillows. She showers and gets dressed and I am still in bed. She goes out into the world to her job while I am at home and all I can think is, "God I love this woman." And I do. She is the love of my life. Her dedication to her job, excellence in her life and those around her, being my lover and my best friend, she truly is amazing. That is not to say that we don't have our disagreements because we do. It has taken a long time, but I think we have reached that place of understanding for each other. I accept her and all that she has to offer and all that she struggles with. She accepts me as I am and asks no more of me other than being true to myself. I love the person that I become when I am with her. She encourages me to not be afraid to dream, but more importantly, to follow those dreams. She is a large part of the reason this book exists. Granted it started out as a type of healing during one of the most trying times our relationship has had to endure, it turned into a story about my life, my journey and those around me, she was and still is my inspiration. I hope that I can give her all that she has given to me, emotionally, mentally and financially.

I have not always been the best at taking care of finances and I have never said that I wanted someone to take care of me. As long as I have known her, she has never let me go without, even when my pride kept me from asking.

Over the years, she has spoiled me on many occasions with lavish gifts that I have never expected from a lover, gifts that I have not been able to reciprocate in dollar value. She is a wonderful provider and she takes care of me in her own special way. I do pride myself on being a pretty independent woman, but I have also found a sense of comfort in knowing that she takes care of me, especially since I am used to being the one who has always been taking care of someone else.

I have younger siblings, which at times made me feel like a surrogate mother. I became a mother at eighteen and then I was living with my future husband at age nineteen. I was used to taking care of everyone else's needs. By twenty-two, I was a wife and had two kids. I did not realize how much I was losing in the path that I had chosen. When those things come to you when you are young, motherhood and marriage, you don't have the opportunity to develop yourself as a person. Now at twenty-six, I am learning so many things about myself, what I like to do by myself, in my free time, what I value in relationships, caring for myself and just being able to have a selfish moment to put my needs first. Things I should have discovered sooner and been able to do without so many complications. I can only speculate about my sexuality and whether or not I would have figured that out had I not been wrapped up in those other things. Don't get me wrong. I love both my girls dearly and they shape a huge part of my identity. Knowing them has made me a better person all around. They have inspired me to continue on my path, no matter how difficult it has been. For them and their gifts of love, squeals of childhood laughter and innocent joy, I am grateful.

Chapter Five

Baby you got a phatty, the type I like to marry
Wantin' to just give you everything and that's kinda scary
Cause I'm loving the way you shake your ass
Bouncin', got me tippin' my glass
Normally don't get caught up too fast
But I got a thing for you
I see you windin' and grindin' up on that pole,
I know you see me lookin' at you and you already know
I wanna love you, you already know
I wanna love you, you already know
-Snoop Dogg, Wanna Love You

This might be my opportunity to be politically incorrect. I once went to a Pride parade in New York City and I met a few nice lesbians and one of them had me wondering. Why do we as women want to come across so hard that we look like men and even act like them? The whole point of being lesbian is that there are no men!! I like the tomboyish girls and I am diggin' the femmes BUT I don't want a woman who acts and tries to look like she has more testosterone than my brother. Then again, what did I say back in Chapter One? Underneath those nice tits and ass is a man. This next selection is called *Fantasies and Fairytales* and I think it highlights a subtle distinction between the femmes and the butches and how we like to get down.

I know we've all been there. You're minding your own business when out of nowhere the finest woman comes along. And I mean FINE. You know, the kind of woman that makes you stop mid sentence, the kind of woman that triggers that wetness in your panties?

There I was at the carwash vacuuming my whip when she pulled up. Honey was blazin'. She opened the door and I watched as one honey colored leg slid out of the Escalade truck. I loved cars and I loved beautiful women so she had my full attention. She hopped out, looked around, and then looked at me.

"You almost done? I'm in a hurry."

"Oh, look at this," I thought to myself. Honey was a diva and had some attitude to top it off.

She walked towards me and I couldn't help but stare at her. She had these long sexy legs wrapped in some booty shorts and I mean booty shorts. She was the color of champagne and lord knows I would have loved to sip on her.

"Yeah, I'll be done in a second. What's your name shorty?"

"Mya."

"It's nice to meet you Mya. I'm Unique. I hope you don't think I am coming on too strong, but I must say, you are a very beautiful woman."

"Thank you. You like what you see?"

All I could do was smile at her. If I didn't know any better, I would say she was checking me out too.

"You're not so bad looking yourself. I like that thuggish look on a sista."

In my mind I was just a regular chick, baby butch if you will, short curly blond hair, green eyes, tight body thanks to Billy Blanks, but I still had those woman curves that seemed to drive most femme chicks crazy.

In the middle of my thoughts, the vacuum stopped working and I snapped back to reality with Mya standing next to me. She reached over for the vacuum and it was as if I had been electrocuted. She smelled so good and she looked so soft.

"Fuck this," I thought to myself. My panties were wet, yes, panties. Butch or not, I still loved my Vickies and I wasn't about to give them up for anything. My clit was waking up and all I could think about was putting on my strap and having her ride it.

"Mya, could I take you out tonight?"

"Think you can handle it?"

"I can handle whatever you got."

She scribbled something on a piece of paper and she handed it to me. She pulled me close and whispered in my ear.

"I know what you want and I plan on giving it to you. I've been watching you for a while and all I could think about was having your tongue and those lips all over my body."

At that moment, I was glad I wasn't of the male persuasion because my dick would have been a brick and I would have had to bend this woman over the hood and tear dat ass up.

She licked my ear and sent me off. I got in my car and drove. I don't know where, I just drove, trying to get my thoughts together about the situation at hand. I looked at the note she gave me. It was her address and a time. "*8 p.m. Don't be late*," it read.

I made it home and I had to relax and prepare for the night's activities. This was the first time a woman had come along and made me lose my cool. I picked out some new gear from my closet and I opted for some boxers instead of the Vickies. She liked a thuggish chick; so a thug was what she was gonna get. The funny thing is, thug or not, the routine is still the same. I showered, shaved up everything, you know, did my girly maintenance. After all that, I got decked out in my Tommy gear and one of my many new pairs of Timberland boots. I know they're always saying they don't make their stuff for black folks, but I could care less. Hilfiger got some nice shit. It makes me look good and ain't nothin' like a new pair of Tims. After checking myself out in the mirror, I splashed on some cologne and I was ready to go.

I grabbed my goody basket along with a bottle of champagne, some strawberries and candles. Yeah, my ass was a playa and I played to win.

I arrived at her house at 7:59 p.m. and rang the doorbell at exactly 8 p.m. When she opened the door, there she stood in a purple teddy with the garter and some black high heels. I stepped inside and I tried to control the throbbing that was starting in between my legs.

"Well hello. You look...dayum girl. Wow."
"I don't want to waste any time...I have been thinking about you all day."

She led me upstairs to her bedroom that was illuminated with candles and there were slow jams playing in the background. The room smelled as delicious as she did. She brought me inside and she closed the door. She turned around to face me and she fell into my arms. She was as soft as I had imagined her to be. I leaned down to kiss her and she hungrily accepted.

My mouth played with hers, softly licking her lips and sucking on her tongue. My hands slid all over her body, which was smooth as silk. I slid a hand under her teddy and reached up to feel her breasts. Her nipples were poked out, saluting me. I rolled one in my fingers and she let out a moan. I picked her up and she wrapped her legs around me and we fell onto the bed. God she smelled so good. I started biting and sucking on her neck and feeling up her thighs. I slid the teddy off her silky body and I had to stand back for a moment to look at her. I could tell she was an exhibitionist because when she saw me looking, she decided to put on a show. She got to her knees and she raised her arms above her head and began moving her body to the music. She was what R. Kelly talked about when he said, "*Move your body like a snake, ma...*" Her breasts stuck out, her nipples inviting me to suck them, taste their sweetness. She had perfectly shaven pubic hair and I just stood there in awe as she slid a finger into herself and began massaging herself and caressing her breasts. I managed to undo my pants and slide out of my boots. I walked over to the side of the bed and the sexy thug in me came out.

"You need some help with that?"

I reached over and slid my hand over hers and took over the rubbing that she had started. She was so wet and I could see her juices glistening in the light. I instinctively began licking my lips. I couldn't wait to taste her. I pushed her down on the bed and I buried my face in her. I kissed her up and down her thighs, caressing every bit of skin along the way until I reached the essence of her and that sweet nasty gushy stuff. I licked her like a tootsie pop, my tongue gliding up and down and in and out of her. This was my thing. There was nothing like the taste of a woman. I wanted to make her cum, drink all she had to offer, and then make her cum some more.

"Oh, I like that…don't stop baby…"

I could feel her clit pulsating in my mouth as it swelled. Her body squirmed underneath me and I devoured her.

"Lick it like that, oh, yeah, shit that feels so…Ummm I gonna,…"

She never finished her sentence as she started to cum. As my tongue darted in and out of her I could taste her sweet juices. I began to suck on her swollen clit, bobbing my head, all the while darting my tongue in and out of her, drinking all the sweetness that poured out. She came over and over, pulling at my hair. When her body started to shake, I released her and I licked a trail up her body, through the valley of her belly, over her breasts, lingering at her nipples, then to her lips.

"You okay?"

"yeah."

"Good, because I'm not done yet."

I reached for my goody basket and I pulled out the strawberries and champagne. I popped open the bottle and I reached for the strawberries. I trailed them along her body, licking off the sweet juices, then fed them to her. I watched her flick her tongue over those berries and I could feel my own juices beginning to flow. I poured champagne in her navel and I licked it out. I poured it over her body and I licked off every drop. My own body was hot and I wanted to get inside of her. I pulled out my strap and she looked at me. There I was naked, my dick ready to attack that ass of hers. She lay down on the bed, legs parted, inviting me to come in. I slid into her. She wrapped her legs around my back. Her breath was heavy and she began to nibble on my ear and whisper to me.

"You feel so good…do it harder, deeper…"

"You want it deeper?"

"Yes…"

I kissed her hard and full on the mouth before I slid out of her and flipped her body over. She arched her back out to me, making more of a curve so our bodies could fit together. I slid into her from the back and I placed my hands on her hips to steady myself as I thrust inside her. We rocked on the bed in rhythm, my crotch slamming into her ass. I nibbled on her back and licked down her spine. I played with her breasts as they hung below her body. We were fused together and I loved every minute of it. I slammed into her, harder and harder and our moans were growing louder. My clit ached and I could feel my body getting ready to explode.

"Mya...damn baby I'm gonna cum..."

Our bodies were pounding into each other and the bed had begun to squeak. My body was tense, my pussy wet and my clit throbbing. I could hear Mya nearing her climax. I could feel her pulling my dick into her, holding and squeezing. I closed my eyes and I started to cum.

"Shiiittt, ahhh, Mya, uuhhhh..."

We came together, our voices drowning out the music in the background. We collapsed on the bed, out of breath. I slid out of my strap and before I had time to recover, Mya was between my legs, her tongue flickering over me like the flame on the candle next to us. She licked me from top to bottom, and then back again. I started to cum again

59

and again and I had to beg her to stop. I pulled her up to me and we kissed for a long time.

"So, tell me, Mya, do you always sex women you meet at the carwash?

"Only the one I met there and fell in love with."

She kissed me on my nose and snuggled herself on my chest. I enjoyed the feel of her silky skin on mine. This was my woman, my love, and my best friend. We kept the passion in our relationship with our little role-play games.

Yesterday I was the doctor getting it on with a patient and today I was the thug at the carwash chasing the honey in the booty shorts. Tomorrow, who knows? Mya knew how to bring this butch to her knees no matter what role we were playing. She was and will always be my femme princess.

Butches, femmes, labels are the biggest bunch of bullshit. We are who we are. I love not fitting into the categories. I love just being me.

<u>Chapter Six</u>

Have you ever tried sleeping with a broken heart?
Well you could try sleeping in my bed...
Why don't you hold me, need me...
I thought you told me you'd never leave me...
-Alicia Keys, Try Sleeping With A Broken Heart

September 5, 2004

I don't know where to begin. My heart is aching, my mind unable to rest. We have been apart for more days than I care to remember and even though we share physical space, you are no longer here with me. Every day I realize that I am in love alone and it is a painful place to be. You look at me, you touch me, I can even make you laugh, but it is not the same for you anymore. You want to reduce me to a friend, but how can that be when I have touched your soul, bathed in the beauty of you, received you into me as one? I feel empty, lost, missing and needing you. You once told me I was a whole person when we met and yes, you were right. I am still a whole person, but a part of me is missing...the part I gave to you...

One of the most painful things I have experienced came from bullshit. I won't call it "Lesbian Bullshit" because that would be unfair. Everyone, gay, straight and in-between is capable of having issues that cause them to be unable to commit, enjoy true intimacy and have long lasting relationships. It's just too bad that these people don't come with red flags attached somewhere so those of us who are ready, willing and able to do the work and have successful ventures do not get sucked into a huge mess with someone who can't. Having a little baggage is certainly ok because no one is drama free, but damn, I can do without the whole set of Luis Vitton.

I call it bullshit because to experience pain, never deal with it, put up walls that hurt people who love us and aren't trying to hurt us is exactly that. To be grown and still running from the childhood boogey-man is just juvenile. You can't go on blaming mommy and daddy forever. Eventually you have to take responsibility. No one wants to be vulnerable and admit to loving or needing another person but if we plan on ever having long-term relationships that are healthy and thriving, we need to open up those doors and tear down the walls that we think are there to protect us.

No man or woman is an island and we all need love. The problem does not lie in falling in love. It comes from maintaining the love when people get really close and issues of commitment arise. There is nothing wrong with eating, sleeping and breathing someone as long as they are doing the same. I can understand fear, but what I can't understand or accept is letting fear run your life and ruin your relationships and hurt people you love. If you have not found the strength and/or courage to face those fears, don't put someone in a position to love you only to find out that you can't return the feelings. Just don't go there. It's not fair.

I suppose it is harder for gays and lesbians to connect and enjoy relationships to their full potential because for one, we have constantly been told these relationships are wrong. Perhaps in our subconscious mind that works against us since we have already been told the relationships go against nature, it is no wonder they would not work out, right? So when things don't work, we throw up our hands, call for the u-haul and go off to the next relationship, never questioning why things went how they did.

What demons came into play? I am sure we might also think that because it is a same-sex relationship, things should move smoothly because we are talking about two people who are the same, right? WRONG. Taking two people with very different ideas, styles, values, etc. and building a relationship takes a lot of work and there has to be compromise. Even though she is a she, just like me, I know the things that make her who she is are a lot different than the things that make me who I am. The important thing is allowing for those differences to exist and to make room for acceptance.

One of my favorite things is to see older couples together because it really gives me hope that I will be able to have that life of happily ever after and it strengthens my belief that it is not just a luxury for straight folks. I once met this one couple that had been together for about thirty years and I was just amazed. I haven't been breathing that long. Of course, I always ask about the secrets to a successful relationship. The answer most given is communication and then being considerate of each other. Seems simple enough, right? If only it were so.

I watch my children playing, so happy and carefree and for the most part, they say what they feel and they do not mask their needs out of any type of fear. Somewhere along the line, the innocent child-like ability to state our intimate needs and wants became an inability in adulthood. Instead, we play games, break hearts, build resentment and damage each other. To tell another person that you love them, to show you care, it means exposing yourself and so many of us, from experiences at home or in the world decided it was safer to keep those thoughts to ourselves, even if it means an internal feeling of loneliness and want or hurting someone as they attempt to be close to us.

"I love you, but not like how I should."

At this point in the end of my relationship and as I am trying to heal, I am still struggling with what that statement means in all of this. How exactly should you love a person and who decided what was the proper way? Shouldn't that be left up to the person being loved? I loved her with every part of me. Maybe she felt bad or like she was doing me an injustice because she did not love me that way, but not because she did not feel it, maybe she just didn't know how. Maybe she didn't know how to receive it. Perhaps we are apart because she could not handle someone loving her so genuinely and unconditionally. Maybe that is what didn't feel right.

If you have never had something and then you experience it, does it immediately feel right, especially if you are used to something else? She often said it felt weird to miss me in her everyday life. It was new to her, that yearning and desire, that vulnerability. I felt it too, but I was ready and familiar. I knew what it was like to ache for someone. Maybe she didn't feel it, but are people going to be madly in love everyday at the same time? I would be lying if I said I never had frustrations or moments where my love was not as strong, but seeing her, hearing her voice revived whatever was waning inside me. We brought out the best parts in each other amidst our flaws and to me, when that happens maybe you do love that person like you should. If you can't be honest, if you are lying, cheating, abusing or disrespecting yourself or each other, then no, you are not loving that someone like you should.

By the time God made woman, He was into the second week of working overtime. An angel appeared and asked, "Why are you spending so much time on this one?"

65

God answered, "Have you seen my spec sheet on her? She has to be able to run on Diet Coke, leftovers, have a kiss that can cure anything from a scraped knee to a broken heart. She heals herself when she is sick AND can work eighteen-hour days."

The angel then noticed something, and reaching out, touched the woman's cheek. "Oops, it looks like you have a leak in this model," the angel said. "I think you're trying to put too much into this one."

"That's not a leak," God corrected, "that's a tear. The tear is her way of expressing her joy, her sorrow, her pain, her disappointment, her love, her loneliness, her grief and her pride."

"Woman is truly amazing," the angel marveled.

"She certainly is! Women have strengths that amaze men. They bear hardships and they carry burdens, but they hold happiness, love and joy. They smile when they want to scream. They sing when they want to cry. They cry when they are happy and laugh when they are nervous. They fight for what they believe in. They stand up to injustice. They don't take 'no' for an answer when they believe there is a better solution. They go without so others can have. They go to the doctor with a frightened friend. They love unconditionally. They cry when their children excel and cheer when their friends get awards. They are happy when they hear about a birth or a wedding. Their hearts break when a friend dies. They grieve at the loss of a family member, yet they are strong when they think there is no strength left."

"They know that a hug and a kiss can help to heal a broken heart. Women come in all sizes, in all colors and shapes. They'll drive, fly, walk, run or e-mail you to show how much they care about you. The heart of a woman is what makes the world keep turning! They bring joy and hope. They have compassion and ideals. They give moral support to their family and friends. Women have vital things to say and everything to give."

"Are there no flaws?" the angel asked.

"Of course. Because nothing can be perfect, each woman will have her unique flaws. But there's one they all have in common. I've tried to get it out of this model, but even I can't seem to fix it."

"What's that?"

"They all tend to forget their worth."

-Anonymous

A friend sent that to me via e-mail when my relationship was crumbling and there were things going on that made a woman's worth come into question. Socialized as nurturers, we are taught and know how to care for everyone except ourselves. We give so much and rarely get anything close in return and that becomes everyday life. Very rarely are we takers even when all we have to give has been taken from us. Being a woman and loving a woman, I marvel at our strength, inner and outer beauty and our ability to keep going when all seems to be lost. We may have been cut from the rib of a man, but our strength, our capacity to love and nurture and survive…that is all our own.

Chapter Seven

I call this one *Last Night*, a story about two people struggling to maintain a relationship even though they are not on equal footing. I wrote this as an expression of my frustration in a situation I was unprepared to deal with. Love was put to the test from day one and this short story chronicles the journey of passion, frustration, heartache and finally understanding. There was drama over the kids, the finances, and living space. Blending lives is no easy task and it is even harder when there are other issues at work. This was the beginning of a painful realization that sometimes love isn't enough. *Read on….*

I love watching you sleep. I always have. It must be the serenity of your cute sleepy look that always allowed me to overlook your snoring. Unlike other nights where watching you sleep would soothe me into my own dreamland, this night was bringing me pain. So many things ran through my mind as I watched you. Feeling the warmth of your body radiate to mine. Whenever I would snuggle up close enough, your arms would instinctively open to receive me. Not tonight though.

Lesbian Bullshyt

In such a short amount of time we shared a lot of love…made love with a passion I had always longed for, but never experienced. Lately that passion had been absent and watching you sleep had become a bittersweet moment. I remember the love we made and longed for it, the untainted love that fueled our conversations, touches, caresses, kisses and sweaty romps in the bed. Our sex was the bomb and we knew it.

"You like that?"

"Yes, baby don't st-stop…"

Our bodies blended together as you nibbled on my ear then licked a trail of fire down my neck. I loved the way those little nibbles felt along with the softness of your lips as they sent little pulses of pleasure up and down my side. You had both my arms pinned down with just one hand and not being able to reach out and touch you was driving me wild. I could feel your kisses going down over my breasts and gently tugging at my nipples. I could hear you and all those sexy noises you were making as you became more and more turned on. As you worked your way down, you released my arms and I closed my eyes and pressed my head into the pillow as you licked your tongue in and out of my navel. I could feel your breath on my thighs when I grabbed for your hair.

"Tell me what you want."

"I want to feel you inside of me."

I was so hot for you and it felt as though my insides were oozing out of me. You put a finger inside of me and I could see you grinning from sheer delight. You slid in another finger, then moved your thumb over my clit and began massaging it. Your strokes were deep and I could feel my body begin to tighten and relax, preparing itself for the climax that would soon follow.

"God that feels so good…"
"Are you wet for me sweetie?"
"Yes, mmmm, that feels good. I want you…"
"Want me to what?"

You were such a prankster. Before I responded, I took a moment to look at you, taking in the sight of you as you slid your fingers out of me, licked your lips, and then buried your face in me. I could feel the warmth of your tongue on me, stroking up and down, then diving in and out of me. I could feel that familiar momentum building up and my clit began to throb, aching to be released of the pressure that had built up there. I arched my back to you, inviting you to release me. You knew exactly what I wanted but you wanted, no, you needed to hear me and I knew you would tease me until I begged. I could feel you moving away from me, the tip of your tongue teasing me, driving me to the edge of ecstasy coupled with the warmth of your breath on my legs. You made your way to my thighs and you kept this up until you got what you needed and my body was ready to explode.

"Baby please! I just want to feel you inside me, underneath me, on top of me…just stop teasing me and make me cum!"

You raised your head up to look at me and I could tell you were on top of the world. You had teased me to the point where I was begging you to release the sexual tension that had mounted in my body. I grabbed your head and raised my hips to meet your hungry lips. I loved the feel of your tongue on my body and it only took you minutes to make me come, and hard.

"You gonna come for me?
"Yes…."

I let out a moan as I answered and I could feel my breathing get heavy, my nipples were hard and my clit begin to throb. You were all over me, licking, tasting and nibbling, drinking me, like a Heineken on a hot day. Suddenly I could feel that familiar feeling and my back arched as I tried to get closer to you. In a flash, all the tension you had placed within me, you set free as I came, calling your name and tugging at your hair. I could hear you reaching your own climax as you listened to me.

"Come for me baby…"

"Uh, right there, yeah, um hmm, Bri!"

In one hand, I had a handful of your hair. In the other, I had clenched sheets. Wave after wave of orgasmic pleasure shot through me and just like I had to beg for you to start, I had to beg for you to stop. You had this way of licking and blowing on me after I had cum a few times to keep things going and eventually, my body would shake and my voice would get hoarse. You always said I made too much noise, but you loved it. You climbed up to my face and I could see your eyes soften with that look of love before you leaned down to kiss me. I could taste myself on your lips. I loved to kiss you. You had the softest lips and every time our lips met, it did things to me.

As we lay there in each other's arms, I could hear you whisper a gentle "I love you" in my ear. I pulled you close to me and whispered the same. I wound up watching you sleep that night with so much love in my heart and at that moment, no one could have ever told me that watching you sleep would bring me pain. But here I am watching you, with nothing but memories like that to console me.

Our relationship was quick. It was as if we met one week and fell in love the next. What wasn't there to love? We fit like two peas in a pod and I often found myself staring at you wondering just where you came from. When I had just about abandoned the idea of someone to love, you came along and rescued my heart from loneliness. It was a chance meeting at Starbucks, the local coffeehouse stashed in Barnes & Noble. I didn't think there was anyone else around who loved caramel frappuchinos and books as much as I did, but the woman ahead of me ordered one and she had an arm full of books. We bumped into each other getting napkins. She had this sexy look about her, her short hair complementing her face and she was just plain hot in her leather jacket and sunglasses. She took off her glasses to introduce herself and she had the softest brown eyes I had ever seen and a beautiful smile. We just struck up a conversation and over frozen coffee, Brienne Tionne Trusseau melted my heart.

You were new to the area, your services having been requested by the state on some huge education project. You were young and successful, but unlucky in love. I had just turned twenty-seven, finished med school, and searching for a residency program, and had issues in my life. With everything that was going on, you gave me a chance. Even when I tried to stay away, you came to me. I fell for you even when I told myself not to. I didn't want to drag you into the mess that was my life. We had conversations that lasted for hours about nothing and everything and to be in your arms was like being in heaven. I felt loved and I felt safe there, but occasionally, my mind would drift to the reality of my life and the problems there.

"What is wrong? I wish there was something I could do."

"Sweetie, I am fine."

"I didn't know fine looked like that. Why won't you tell me what has you so stressed? If you need help, ask for it."

That was the first time my ego had ever been busted. I was used to being the helper and never the one being helped. I had made some bad choices in my life in the past few months and my biggest downfall was mediocre grades in my last semester of school. I graduated with my class as an M.D., but I could not find a hospital anywhere that would take me into their residency program without me repeating my last semester and bringing my grades up first. I couldn't afford another semester of school, but I needed the schooling if I was to ever make any money to live.

I was a doctor who couldn't practice medicine and my savings account was dwindling quickly. You stepped in and cushioned the huge fall I was about to take. You basically took care of me and my kids while I went back to school. For once, I could actually study and take the time to be a good student. Somewhere along the line, we wound up living together and while you worked, I used my extra time around the house, turning it into a happy home, or so I thought. To you, it was a process that erased your identity.

Lesbian Bullshyt

Midway through the semester, I was offered a spot in a mediocre program that I had absolutely no interest in and when I refused it, you started to change. I had no idea of the bigger changes that were to come. One afternoon, after you had just finished paying bills online, you seemed in a foul mood. When I asked about it, you seemed distant.

"Sweetie, what's on your mind?

"I don't want to get into it right now."

"No, what's up? You've been acting like something has really upset you for the past few days now."

"When you didn't take that residency, it was a slap in the face. I pay for everything in here and you know that and when you had the opportunity to help, you passed it up because it wasn't good enough."

"It's not that it wasn't good enough, it's not what I wanted."

"What about what was needed? Did that matter? I never had any plans for taking care of a family and I feel like that is exactly what I am doing here and I don't like it."

"You always talk to me like I am some bum on the street who never had anything and just latched onto you. I know about the finer things in life, working hard, and making it to the top. You met me when I was down and out and all I had to offer was me. You knew about my kids, you knew I wasn't working and you knew about my problems with school and finances. Yes, I had drama, but you knew. Now you're using that against me, telling me I disrespected you when I passed up a job.

Never mind that I was busting my ass at school, around the house and for you, for us. Whatever happened to 'contribute to the house what you can."

"I meant that…"

"Well obviously, my contribution is not enough because all I am hearing about these days is money. I don't make as much money as you. I am not a big time professor who only works three days a week, contracted by the state and making six figures. I am a single mom in a grueling residency program spending most of my money on daycare because their father is a deadbeat, my family won't help me because they don't like my chosen life and my partner basically wants nothing to do with the responsibility of kids, having a family, etcetera."

"How can you say that? I never said I wanted nothing to do with kids. I care about those two kids and I have love for them, but they are not mine."

"And you are always so quick to make sure I never forget that. Brienne, if I even ask you to pick them up or spend the day with them while I work, you start pouting and all I hear about is the free time you lost. Sometimes I look at you and I wonder exactly what comes to your mind when you hear the word 'family'. Is that something you run away from on purpose or just when it comes to me? I want someone who wants to be there like that for me instead of feeling cramped and violated. Support me like I support you. I have not closed any parts of me from you and I am open to anything that may come our way. It is becoming painfully obvious that my life, my needs in a relationship are very different from yours. I want a partner in every sense of the word, someone who will love me and my children, understand and accept that there can be no "us" without them and be open to having a family with a responsibility that includes raising kids. I am a single parent, so of course I would be looking for those things in a partner. I don't want to play house or the late night visitor game. It's not fair for you to try to have your cake and eat it too."

"I told you…"

"Yeah, yeah, I know, you aren't good with kids. You ever think that maybe it's because you don't want to be? I am really disappointed in you because from what I know of you, every other challenge or opportunity in your life, you tackled and overcame. Things that didn't work, you made work because you wanted them to. You want the benefits of me loving you, but you don't want the responsibility that comes with a relationship with me."

"Nessa, I just feel like I have lost me and the person I was."

"Don't you realize that when you join your life with someone, there are things that you have to sacrifice? I used to stay up all night on the Internet. My free time was spent in front of my computer and in chat rooms. When I started living with you, I stopped doing that. I was a homebody who hardly ever went out. Now, I spend more money on restaurants and worrying about the social skills of my children than I ever did. I used to do lots of things that I don't anymore because they aren't beneficial to the relationship and I do some other things that I never used to do because they are. I realize what a rare and precious thing it is to come across someone who truly loves and cares about you and I am willing to put in work to nurture that relationship. I was looking to settle down and grow old with someone. I thought you were too. I guess I wrong."

"What about me?"

"Oh here we go."

"What is that supposed to mean?"

"It means that the focal point of your life is you. You are so self-involved all you can see is you. Brienne, if you feel that you lost parts of yourself because of this relationship, why don't you just say goodbye? You don't seem to be okay with the fact that with any relationship you do compromise some parts of yourself to gain something deeper. I gave up my space, some of my freedom to be wild and reckless, I had to become mindful of someone else's feelings, but I gained love, a friend and a partner. The way I see it, what I have gained is far more important than what I supposedly lost. I love you and I love the concept of us. That is my focal point, not you and not me, but us. No matter what else is going on in my life, I have never denied you. I work more than one hundred hours a week, sometimes forty-eight hours straight and when I come home, as dead tired as I am, I find time and energy for you. I accept that relationships take work and they require time. Not free time when you have it but time always just like working, studying and playing. You are just as important to me as work, school, my kids. Everything in our relationship seems to be on your schedule. We talk on the phone when you're in the mood, we play around when you're in the mood and we even have sex when you're in the mood. I can't remember the last time you actually came at me aggressively. When I approach you, I get the million and one excuses, 'I'm tired, I'm not in the mood, I have a headache, my stomach is a little upset.'"

"I am not a sex toy."

"This isn't about being a sex toy, it's about trying to connect, to be close. You spend more time telling me 'no' and dwelling on all that is wrong in our relationship. You keep rejecting me and any possibility of a future for us and why? Because I refused the first residency that came along and you felt slighted because you were taking care of a family. You knew my situation when you met me, when you started dating me and when you got serious with me. What the fuck ever happened to for better for worse, richer or for poorer? Or is that just another one of those luxuries for the straight folks?"

"We're not married."

"Yeah, and I can tell just how committed to this relationship you are."

"I can't deal with you or this conversation right now. I'm going out for a ride."

"Whatever, go ahead. All you ever do is run away from the problems your money can't fix."

"Fuck you Vanessa."

"Sometimes, I wish you would."

You stormed out of the kitchen and slammed the front door as you left. This was our life nowadays. We fought about money, space, my feelings, your time, my kids and even their deadbeat dad. Even though I was a budding doctor, my life was a mess. Vanessa Nichols, M.D. I performed surgeries and sometimes saved the lives of strangers, but I couldn't save my own. Because of all my problems, you sometimes treated me like I was nothing, while you used your money to fix every problem you came up against. With two kids, wicked student loans and bad credit, I did not have that luxury. I worked to survive and for you, working was a slight inconvenience. You spent money like water and you lived a fast paced life that was slowed by a girlfriend with kids and drama. I could not travel like you, spend like you or live like you and that cramped your style. You weren't ready to identify with a family. You wanted to live single, but still come home to someone. Instead of being there for me emotionally through these tough times, you just wanted to do away with me, separate yourself from the madness, I suppose. You no longer wanted to live with me, but you wanted to continue our relationship. We were battling daily over the issue. I could not get you to see why I felt that you were being selfish, and that you wanted to have your cake and eat it too. So far, you were behaving like a spoiled child who would not act right until they got their way. You had been using my love for you and sex as a weapon, teasing me here and there, but never allowing yourself to get lost in us. I felt as though you were handing me scraps of you, starving my love for you so even if I did leave, there would be nothing left of us.

It hurt to see you so unhappy with me, especially over something that I felt in my heart, no…I KNEW in my heart was trivial. You simply did not want to let go of your vision of the single, irresponsible you, free to roam for the slower life of wife n' kids. You wanted the best of both worlds and you were going to deny everything about us until you got what you wanted. When I met you, you were living this bachelor life, eating froot loops for dinner, sleeping on the couch and clubbing it three or four nights a week. You came home to shower, change and sleep. I tried to turn a house into a home and I thought you welcomed that. Before I started my residency, I was home and had free time. I cooked, cleaned, ran errands for you, dropped off and picked up dry-cleaning, even remembering to ask for extra starch. I turned into a domestic house bitch for you, because I loved you and I was trying to contribute what I could to the house - myself, my labor, my time. How many evenings had you come in to find a hot meal on the table waiting for you, a fire in the fireplace and open arms waiting for you? I know I couldn't pay half the bills, but I gave you ALL of me. I opened my heart to you, shared my soul and my body with you. I shared my secrets with you, my fears, and my fantasies, my hopes and dreams. I shared me with you. All I ever wanted was for you to give me the same type of love. You had a partner, someone supporting you, in your corner and down for whatever life may have thrown at you. I took our relationship serious. I committed myself to you and the idea of us. I would be there through thick and thin, for better or for worse. To me, marriage was a commitment in someone's heart and soul, not on a piece of paper and I was willing to share that with you.

It was after three in the morning when I heard your motorcycle roaring down the street and eventually pulling up into the garage. You had been gone all night, to the bar no doubt, drinking and shooting pool. Funny thing is, I loved to watch you shoot pool. You had this way of sticking out your butt to make the perfect shot and to see that nice booty always turned me on. I couldn't play to save my life, but I think I purposely remained a poor player so I could watch you lean over the table. I loved you and there were so many little things that I cherished about our relationship and I didn't want to lose that. I didn't want to lose you. I hated the way we were destroying our relationship and our love for each other.

By the time you got upstairs to our bedroom I had turned on the lights and sat up in bed.

"Did I wake you?"

"No, I was up anyway. I couldn't sleep."

There was an awkward silence for a while as I watched you, trying to hide the lust in my eyes as you undressed and slipped into bed. I loved everything about you. Even the body that you swore had too many imperfections. I had to shake my head as I thought about you, the woman who had no idea just how sexy she was and how much she had it going on.

"About earlier…"

"Shhh. I don't want to talk about that. I have been thinking and I don't want to hurt you, I don't want us to fight like this, but I don't know what to do. Everything in our relationship moved so fast and there was so much going on with you, the kids, and finances. I love you and I want to be with you, but I need some space to work things out within myself. Vanessa, you are a wonderful woman, one of the best things that have ever happened to me and I truly love you and the kids and all I am asking, no begging you, please give me this time to myself. There will still be an "us" unless you don't want there to be one.

"Brienne, I just don't understand, that's all. How can you look at me and tell me you love me and want to be with me, yet you can't share space with me? What kind of future does that leave us with? I don't want to spend the rest of my days living alone or with you coming over when you have nothing else to do or when it's merely convenient. I had that experience and I am past it. I want to settle down and do the family thing. I want that moment where I get to say everyday, "honey, I'm home," and I want someone who wants to come home to me and doesn't mind kids running up to them for hugs and kisses."

"I feel cramped. I never had the chance to live alone. It has always been with a girlfriend or a roommate. I want to ease into the family role and like this, I can't do it. It's instant family."

"It will always be that. My kids and myself are a package deal. That won't ever change. I just want you to be happy. I'd like us all to be happy. The tension in this house is unbearable sometimes and I feel like you look at me like you wish I would go away every time I come through the door."

"Nessa, I wish you could understand."

"I wish you could understand too.

I rolled over and turned out my light and as I lay there in the darkness replaying the conversation over and over in my mind, tears began to fall from my eyes. In my mind, we had a nice life together, the way we talked and laughed and played around. We had a higher level of communication and understanding that was non-existent in my previous relationships. We were friends as well as lovers. I enjoyed having someone around who wanted to fall asleep with me at night and loved waking up to me in the morning. I had someone to cook for who appreciated my efforts. Breakfast on the weekends was our thing and you loved my cooking. What would happen to those things? Why would you want to give up those things to be alone? I felt so rejected and so unloved as I lay there, thinking and quietly venting my pain through my tears.

After a while, I felt you roll over and prop yourself up so you could see my face. You wiped my tears away and put your arms around me.

"Why are you crying?"

"It hurts. I feel like you are rejecting me. The life I have to offer to you is not good enough. I know you want equality, but I want equity."

"I just want to live alone, have time to myself. I am not saying that I don't want you, because I do. I wish you could see that the two things are separate issues. My love for you has nothing to do with this."

"Then why is everything else about us so strained? We hardly talk without getting into these heated debates, we barely make love and then when we do, it feels like a chore. I already feel like you don't want me, you don't want my kids and this is the icing on the cake."

"Okay, I haven't been feeling real sexual lately, but that is the stress and this situation. I feel like nowadays, all you want me for is sex and there is so much pressure for me to put out."

"Brienne, this has nothing to do with putting out. I miss the closeness of us. We had such a deep level of intimacy in our relationship, the way we talked all the time, we flirted, and we just enjoyed each other. It wasn't about sex. That was never our focus. We just wound up that way. I miss us winding up that way and I miss our closeness. You used to talk to me, tell me that you felt you could tell me anything without fear of my reaction. You trusted me with the deepest parts of you. I know you hold back. You don't trust me anymore, not with you."

"I know this is off the subject, but are you off tomorrow?"

"Yeah, why?"

"I was just wondering because it is almost five in the morning and we should be getting some sleep. Not that I am trying to put you off or anything, I just want you to be rested."

"I know and I appreciate that. I am off for the next few days. In case you hadn't noticed, I have worked the last twelve days straight."

"Yes, I did notice and I don't know how you do it. I am amazed at your strength sometimes. You are a good mother to those kids and I know you work hard and give a lot to this relationship and I know I take you for granted. I don't mean to and it has been so easy for me to get used to you just being here that I forget about the work of keeping you here in my life. I don't want that to become a habit and I want to work on things for myself so I can be a better girlfriend, a better partner. I think the space will be good for us both, help us get back what we had. Before we lived together, we took time for each other and now, we just blend into each other. Space doesn't mean the end of us."

"I miss blending with you..."

Lesbian Bullshyt

The sun was just beginning to rise outside and I could see the reflection in your eyes. I could also see that you wanting to live alone had nothing to do with love for me because at that moment, there was so much love in your eyes. You reached over to caress my cheek and I instinctively closed me eyes. Your touch always soothed me. You leaned over to kiss me and I kissed you back. The next thing I knew, we were rolling around in the bed kissing each other, biting and sucking as if it was the first time in a long time.

"Nessa, mmmm, I'm sorry for hurting you. God you feel so good. I'm going to love you better, just give this a chance...."
"Bri..."

I could barely get words out of my mouth because of your lips pressed to mine. I decided to close my eyes and just enjoy the feel of you and the blending of our bodies. Somewhere along the line, you must have strapped up because I could feel you sliding into me and I dug my nails into your back. You stopped for a moment to give my body a chance to remember the feel of you. We rocked together, exploring each other as the sun came up. We made love for what seemed like hours, recapturing what we had lost over the last few months and resolving to be better people, lovers and partners. Eventually, our physical love making ceased and we snuggled up to each other. You fell asleep on my chest and I just watched you. I wrapped my arms tight around you and enjoyed the moment. As I lay there, I thought about everything we had been through. There was no pain as I watched you sleep, only fond memories of last night and making love with you and strengthening our commitment to each other and our relationship.

Things worked for a minute, but soon after if was more of the same. I couldn't handle it so I broke off my formal relationship with Vanessa. I still loved her but I couldn't handle the way things were changing, yet staying the same. We still lived together, but I was looking to leave. I needed a fresh start, but I was having a hard time letting go.

We were so close and I worked so hard to deny my feelings because I did not want to be in a relationship where I felt burdened or like I was the only one capable of taking care of things on a financial level. Vanessa was trying, but things just weren't changing. What a mess things turned out to be.

October 17, 2004
I had to go searching through the archives to find this email. Wanted to say hi, maybe even surprise you a little bit with an email from me. HAHAHA. This morning has not been so good and as usual, it is more of the same. In the world according to Terri, it is not the same thing to spoon, kiss and cuddle, as it is to actually have sex. For some reason, those things are on a different plane. One is okay for friends, the other is

not, but to people like you and me, they are on the same level and certainly not for friends. I feel like I am going crazy and everyday I am living some sort of lie that I am unable to escape. And I love this fool and I am just as much a fool for loving her. I feel so stupid.
It is so important to know who you are and to have boundaries.

I was horrible when it came to Brienne and boundaries. I was in love with her and we still shared the same bed even though our formal relationship was over. What could I say? I had no experience in things like that. We fought, we cried, we made up, but never got back together, I felt like she was dangling me on a string. Eventually I got tired and I said no more. It took me a while but I learned to say no and walk away. I could accept it if she just didn't love me anymore but to admit to loving me, share a bed, a life and a home, but still deny the bond that we had…that was just too much to bear.

Keep on walkin', I ain't talkin' to ya anymore…
-CeCe Peniston, KeepOn Walkin'

Chapter Eight

"Feels like I just walked right out of heaven,
feels like I done damn near thrown my life away...
don't know what to do to get back right with you..."
-JAGGED EDGE Walked Outta Heaven

It is sad that she had to lose me before she could appreciate my place in her life.

I pulled into the lot of Barnes & Noble and quickly found a parking space. I sat in the car for a moment to gather my thoughts. I was so tired and beat. I had been working and studying, practically killing myself to finish my doctorate so I could make some money. Well, no, it was more than the money. I made enough of that, if there was such a thing. I guess my drive to make it was the approval that I never got as a kid. Even though I knew better, there I was, thirty-three years old, still trying to win the unconditional love that had been denied to me. I don't know why I thought this degree would be any different than the last two. Oh well. All I wanted right now was a nice latte to wake me up so I could finish the rest of my paper. I got out of the car and I headed for the door. Once inside, I took in the familiar surroundings, the books, the quiet noise and the faces there. I loved big bookstores. There was something about being surrounded by knowledge that made me feel like I belonged. Part of the appeal was the Starbucks Coffee too. As I approached the café, my heart jumped into my throat. I was staring at the woman who had reached into my heart, kissed my soul and touched my very being. I loved her, I really did, but I was too wrapped up in me. I had issues I needed to deal with and when she pressed me, I blamed it on so many things about her. She got fed up and she left me. I was too stubborn to fix it or open my mouth and ask her to stay.

I tried to hurry past the table she was sitting at, but I couldn't help but stare at her. She looked beautiful. She was young and vibrant and I had the pleasure of watching her grow into what she would call a "girly thug." Her look was rugged, yet feminine and she had these full, succulent lips that I tried hard not to remember kissing. I watched her playfully turn the pages of her book, her eyes eagerly following the words. She had cut her hair very short and it fit her so well, bringing out her face and eyes. She had a look of sophistication and gentle sexiness, nothing too overpowering, but just right for her.

We would sit and talk for hours, she and I. She practically hung off my every word. I never had a woman love me like that and I have to admit, when I had it, I didn't appreciate it. Now that it is gone…well, I can't dwell on that and I know you know how it goes. This was the first time our paths had crossed in the many months since we broke up. She was looking forward to spending time with me and building back our relationship but I just couldn't get pass the past. We broke up before our one-year anniversary and she was devastated.

"What can I get for you today?"

The girl behind the counter snapped me out of my dreamland.

"I'd like a vanilla latte with an extra shot of vanilla and an extra shot of espresso. As a matter of fact, make that two shots."
"Wow, two shots? Somebody is hittin' it hard these days."

I knew that voice but I was too afraid to turn around. I didn't want her to see that I still loved her and I definitely didn't want to look at her and see the same look she had when she walked out.

I met her in this little café and there were so many memories. She used to tell me how whenever she came alone, the staff would always ask about her missing "friend". I guess people just expected to see us together all the time, because we were always together. Before we broke up, she told me she had come in here alone, order coffee and sit at a table and she would just cry. This was the place where we had met and back then our relationship was dying like the leaves on the trees. And just like that was a part of nature and the seasons changing, the end of our relationship was beginning to seem natural too. I seemed to be plagued by relationship cancer and whenever I got together with someone, the relationship only had six months to a year to live. After ten months, my relationship with her was about dead and we hadn't yet decided if it was DNR. Do Not Resuscitate.

She was young, she had some baggage, but no more than the next person, she had kids and I know it makes me sound horrible, but no matter how much I loved her, I just couldn't or wouldn't deal with her kids. I was so stuck on not being ready for parenthood, I couldn't just enjoy the experience. I was so worried about being bad at it and somehow damaging them, I couldn't see that I was actually doing okay and that my holding back would be the thing that did real damage. She wasn't asking me to adopt them or anything like that and, most times they were fun. I didn't like having my things broken, but I was harsh. The ironic thing is, I spent so much time fussing over all that was material in my life, and then I lost it all when my condo caught fire. I got a nice fat check from the insurance company and the condo association and I can repurchase newer, better stuff, but I am sure it would be much harder to fix the damage that was done while I was arguing about what was broken. I miss those kids, but I could never tell her that. Just the same way that I couldn't tell her about the nights I couldn't fall asleep because I missed her so much, but I was the one who wanted her out of my house. I wanted to live alone and I needed my space. I put her through a lot of unnecessary shit and I know she hurt because of me. Now here she was, waiting for me to turn around, looking happier than I had ever seen her.

"Can I get a venti white chocolate mocha with extra whipped cream please?"

"Sure, I'll get that for you right now."

I turned around to face her and she still took my breath away. She looked great. As I stared into her eyes it was as if our life together flashed before me. I could see our first meeting, our first date, the first time I kissed her. God I loved her. She had this passion for life. She was wild and reckless, almost a thug sometimes. She was Vanessa Nichols, M.D.

She worked hard for those two letters after her name. So much about her had changed, yet so much was the same. She still had that fire in her eyes and I wanted to put my arms around her, hold her, pour out my heart and soul to her, but she would never listen, never believe. Here we were in a public place with so many people. I would never behave as if I were anything more than her casual friend because that's all I ever did, even when we were lovers. I was too worried about what other people would think to even hold her hand. She hated that because it made her feel like I was ashamed of her or like being in the closet. Heaven knows we all work too hard to get out, to have someone trying to shove us back in.

Lesbian Bullshyt

"How have you been?"

"Good. You?"

"I can't complain. I finally finished up my residency requirements and the doors of life are finally opening for me."

"Sounds good. I am happy for you."

"How's the PhD going?"

"Still going. I have been working on my dissertation. That's why I need two shots of espresso these days." That and the fact that I have not had a good night's sleep since you left."

"I heard about your condo."

"Yeah, well, at least now I don't have to worry about selling the place."

Beep, beep, beep..."Oh, that's my pager. Excuse me."

"Sure."

I watched her whip out her cell phone and make her call. For some reason, I felt like such a loser standing there. I had a nice job, I was a PhD candidate, I had no bills, I just had a vacation in Hawaii, but I did not have that glow like Nessa. She was happy and carefree. This woman would have done anything for me and I let her slip away. She finished her conversation and she walked over towards me.

"Hey, I have to get going, but it was nice seeing you though."

She tapped me on my side, waved, spun around and then she was gone. I watched her leave the store and get into her car. The Honda that I remembered had been replaced by a BMW. She always said she would get one when she made it to the top and money was no longer an issue.

I stood there for a while, sipping my latte, then decided to head out. I reached into my pocket for my keys and out slipped a piece of paper. I looked at it only to realize it was Vanessa's handwriting. I don't know how or when she managed to slip me a note, but there it was. I began to read it aloud.

"Just because someone smiles it doesn't mean they are happy. 555-7272."

She had given me her number. Had she looked at me and been able to read my feelings like a book? Even if she did, who cares? I was tired of hiding behind so much. No one cared about the intricacies of my life. T hey had their own dramas to tend to. I loved and missed her. In less than a month, I would have my PhD. I was a professor, I worked a few days a week, traveled, had money, but every night when I came home, the only thing waiting for me was the TV. Most of my friends had settled down into life with their partners.

"Girlfriends were what we had when we were in our 20s," they would say. Now they wanted people to live with, grow old with, and maybe even do the kid thing.

You can't imagine how I felt, knowing I had all that and I sent it away. I will never forget that last night, when Vanessa left.

"Brienne, when are you going to get some counseling?"

"I am not going to counseling. Those issues aren't important right now."

"Oh, so I guess we aren't important right now since I am the one who brings up those issues. It doesn't matter how much anyone tries to love you because you don't love yourself. How often do you stand in the mirror and scrutinize the woman that you see? How often do you try to mold yourself into what you think the people around want you to be?"

"You don't know me."

"You're right, I don't know you, and I never could because you don't even know who you are. You're too busy to find out and I'm tired of trying to rescue you from the abyss of loneliness. No place stops you from being who you are, you are the only person who does that."

"Who are you to sit and counsel me? I don't have time for this. We keep having these conversations that go in circles and we don't get anywhere."

"You know why we don't get anywhere? You refuse to let go. You keep telling the same tired sob story about how the world needs to understand your plight and no one really wants to hear it. Things happened, you were hurt, or mistreated. Don't you think it's time to get over that? You met me, I had kids, and you fell in love with me. You started school, you never even thought to talk to me about what strains that would put on our relationship. I had just moved out and we never even talked about that. Life just went on for you and I was left to deal with the hurt. You never even acknowledged my pain. As long as you were comfortable, life was grand. Supposedly, you love me and you care, yet you keep telling me I would be happier with someone else. And on top of that, I think you're selfish. All you care about is you, your stuff, how good it looks, how much it costs and all that. You put me and my kids through hell living with you in this virtual museum."

"Why can't you just let me be? Let me live my life."

"Oh, I am going to let you do just that because you are a battery drainer. I am tired of these stupid cat and mouse games. I am gone Brienne, gone like the wind. Until you find yourself and get your priorities straight, lose me from your memory."

With that, she turned around and walked out the door. Since I had already basically put her out, she didn't have anything to move, no reason to come back and she never did. At first, I didn't think she was serious.

Lesbian Bullshyt

We had these little spats before and she always came back to mend things.

After a week without a word from her, I went on about my business. I was glad to be free from the responsibility of a serious relationship. Now I could go out, work out, study, travel, and just be me with no questions asked. That lasted for a good month and a half, and then I missed her. The sound of her voice, her touch, her smile and everything about the way she loved me. She took the time to be there for me, no matter what was going on. I realized she was right. She being in my life did not stop me from doing the things I had always done. The fact was, my love for her made me want to stay with her all the time and I was not used to that, to needing and wanting someone how I wanted and needed her. No matter how much I missed her, I refused to admit what I felt, to pick up the phone and call and I never went by her house to see if she was there. I had school to keep me busy and I read some nights until I could hardly keep my eyes open and when that didn't work, there was always a nice bottle of gin to help me forget. I managed to drown out the pain that I felt and accomplished an important goal at the same time.

One night, I went out to the convenience store to grab a box of Froot Loops and I saw Vanessa's ex husband with the kids. They were walking back to his car and even though they weren't facing me, I would know those two kids anywhere. I was flooded with such emotion that it scared me. I loved those two and there was nothing I could say to the person they were with. He had caused enough drama, but yet it was his right to be with them when he chose. It's ironic how I could see how he only came around when it was convenient, but I could not see that same behavior in myself. I am sure Vanessa would have let me spend time with the kids, but that wasn't something I was ever really interested in. I spent more time trying to distance myself from them instead of simply returning the love and hugs her kids showered on me. At that moment though, I was upset. That deadbeat was playing dad for a minute because it must have been convenient. Tomorrow he would forget all about having kids. I was angry by the time I made it back to my house. So angry, I did something I had not done in years. I sat down in front of the fireplace and I just cried. I cried for those two kids and for my behavior towards them. I cried for the love I had lost. Cried for myself and all the pain I held onto my whole life that kept me from being happy and sharing myself with someone, and I cried because it just plain felt good to let all of that shit out of my soul.

I must have fallen asleep because when I woke up, the fire was out and it was morning. After sitting on the couch and staring at the phone, I dialed the number that Vanessa had given me. After a few rings, a familiar female voice answered.

"Hello?"

"Hi Jo-Jo, may I speak to Vanessa please?"

"Sure. Mommy, phone!"

I heard the phone being placed down and voices in the background. After a few seconds, another voice came on the line.

"Hello?"

"Vanessa?"

"Oh, Brienne, hi, how are you?"

"I'm good. How's it going?"

"Not too bad. I just got home from the hospital. I did my first major surgery last night."

"Congratulations. I know that must have been exciting for you."

"Yeah, it has been very exciting, very fast paced. A lot has changed in the last few months."

"I see, or I should say, I saw. Nice car."

"That's my new baby. I picked it out."

I couldn't take the polite conversation anymore. Inside I felt as though my soul was going to explode if I did not tell this woman what I had learned about myself and what I felt for her. I wanted to hear more about her life, her new journeys and experiences. I just wanted to be a part of her intimate life again.

"Nessa…I don't mean to interrupt you, but there is something I need to tell you."

"What's that?"

"I miss you, I miss us, I miss the kids. My life has not been the same since you left."

"It wasn't supposed to be the same. It was supposed to be better for you."

"Nessa, I have made some mistakes and my biggest one was letting you slip away."

"Brienne, the past is the past. You can't change it, so why dwell on it?"

"I want to change the future. Right now, I only see one thing in my future and that is a PhD."

"Isn't that what you…"

"Wait a minute", she interrupted, "let me finish. I see a PhD, a nice house with a yard, two-car garage, and I see me, but I don't see you. I miss you and I…I need you and I am not afraid of that anymore. I miss knowing that you loved me and would be there. I have been working hard on fixing me and letting go of the hurt so I could love."

"I don't know what to say. I was angry with you for a long time after I left. I just couldn't forgive you for not taking time for us and then when you just let me leave, it was hard for me to believe that I was ever anything than a passing experience for you."

"I wanted to stop you, I just couldn't move. I didn't know what to say, what to do, how to act. I needed you in a way that I didn't understand and that scared me. I buried myself in my studies, made it so I never had to think about anything except this doctorate. I saw Derek out with the kids last night and that really bothered me. I actually felt a sense of possession, like he had no right. I was a better parent than he."

"Brienne, why now? Is it because it's cold outside? You lost your condo and you're looking for comfort?"

"Okay, I deserve that."

"Yes, you do. I loved you. I looked at you and I saw my past, present and future, my best friend, my lover…my partner. I worked so hard to get my life together so I could be your equal. I wanted to give you a home to come to, a warm place to snuggle. Everything about me, you pushed away for your clubbing, your friends, your travel, then finally your books. And you know me. I am not knocking education. I'm a doctor and I can't do that, but if I could find a balance with school, kids, residency, myself and you."

"I did not push you away. Look, I don't want to argue."

"There is nothing to argue about. You are where you wanted to be. You have made choices to ensure that you would live the life that you want. That's all that ever mattered to you."

"You mattered to me."

"I mattered to you when it was convenient."

"Vanessa, please. Give me a chance."

"I gave you two years of chances and plenty of tears. No more. Not one more day of uncertainty in my life."

With that, she hung up the phone. I sat there stunned. Life is full of irony. When I had choices and options, I couldn't make up my mind. She wanted to be with me and she waited. She was hurt because of me. I told her I didn't want her or the life we had. I needed and wanted more things. I was all she ever wanted, plain and simple. Now that I didn't have any choices, it was as clear as day to me what choice I wanted to make. Unfortunately, my choice was no longer a willing option and who could blame her?

I stepped into the bath and the room was filled with steam. The hot water cascaded over my body, caressing me. All I could think of was HER. The hot beads of water searing my skin triggered memories of her kisses. Her lips would send pulses of electricity through my body, literally turning it on. As I leaned into the water I closed my eyes. I had done this to myself. There I was in my shower missing this woman. She haunted my days and possessed my nights. Everywhere I went and in almost everything I did I had thoughts of her. I wanted her in a way I never had before and the funny thing is, she used to tell me this moment would come but I never believed her.

I was not willing to succumb to feelings like this but now it seemed I had no choice. My mind, my body, and my heart would not let me run anymore. I wanted her. No, I NEEDED her and I could admit that. Even though I had everything else in my life coming together, I still did not feel whole. I moved away, dated other people, buried myself in my work, but could never find that feeling of peace that I had when I was with her. It's too bad I couldn't admit it or accept it back then. I spent so much time being afraid that I lost out on a wonderful experience. What would she do? I know her. Vanessa was a fighter and she always fought for us and told me I never did. She was right all the time except for this one. She was the one I had been waiting for my whole life but I was too blind to see it.

I cut my shower short and hopped out. I had a plan to put into action. I could not sit back and do nothing. Vanessa taught me that. I loved her and her children and I wanted to spend my life with them and have a real family.

Chapter Nine

Weren't you the one who said that you don't want me anymore
And how you need your space and give the keys back to your door
And how I cried and tried and tried to make you stay with me
And still you said your love was gone and that I had to leave
Now you're Talking bout a family... Now you're saying I complete your dreams
Now you're sayin' I'm your everything... You're confusing me
What you saying to me, don't play wit me, don't play wit me
Cause....
What goes around comes around... What goes up must come down
Now who's cryin', desirin' to come back to me
-Alicia Keys, Karma

It took a long time to recover from the hurt that I felt. Brienne had dragged me through the mud with all of her uncertainty about loving me and wanting to have me in her life as a lover and a partner. I take some of the blame though, because I allowed her to do it. I stayed when I should have gone far, far away from her. It really ate away at my esteem. I had worked hard to get where I was, to feel comfortable in my own skin, to build myself back up and feel like I was worthy of someone wanting to take a chance and spend her life with me. Now that I am on my feet, finally got those two letters after my name (M.D.), my money right, and the three-letter car in the driveway (BMW), now she wants to be with me. I was so mad that I had started talking to myself.

The nerve of that woman! Even to this day, all she thinks about is her image. I guess now I am a woman she can show off to her friends.

"Fuck her," I said out loud.

"Girl, who was that on the phone?"

"That was Brienne. After all this time, she's coming at me talking about she wants to be a family."

"I see she got you all red in the face."

"Whatever."

"She loves you and you know it, but you too busy holding onto that anger. Let it go."

"Let it go? You are actually telling me to let it go? Come on Monica. After all she put me through with her loves me, loves me not, want you, but don't want to live with you bullshit? That woman would have to damn near walk on water to get back into my heart."

"Well, I think Moses is here."

"What are you talking…"

I had turned to look at my friend and finish my sentence but I was cut short when the doorbell rang. I could see through the window that it was Brienne. I know all the color must have drained out of my face. How did she know where I lived? It was always so hard for me to stay mad at her when she showed up. She looked so good. I was so into her and she knew it back then, but I would be damned if I let her know it now. Being a doctor had taught me to mask my feelings.

"Are you going to answer the door?"

I took a deep breath, looked up at the ceiling and went towards the door.

"Girl, I'm just gonna slip out the back."
"Now see, you ain't right, but that's ok. You go ahead. I got this."

With that, my best friend Monica found her way out the back door. For the longest time she had been advocating for Brienne, somehow understanding her plight by also being a woman with no kids. Unlike Brienne though, Monica managed to understand and make room for the differences in our lives. I used to tease her all the time that she should hop the sexuality fence and get with me since all the men in her life seemed to be stuck on stupid. She was my ace and we had been through a lot. She picked me up and put me back together when Brienne broke me.

"I'll call you later. Try not to be so bitter this time."
"Whatever. I got one word for you...Karma."

Monica left and I turned my attention to the front door. Brienne rung the bell twice and I could see her out on my steps fidgeting. I wonder what she was thinking. I see she had grown bold over time. Showing up like this certainly was not her style. But then again, holding all the cards and playing them was not mine. It was hard for me to be mean and nasty but there are times when I think that is necessary so people don't mistake your kindness for weakness. I loved her still, but I would be damned if she would keep dangling me on a string. For once, it would be my way or the highway. I was now in a position to call the shots. I was a doctor in a successful practice making six figures, had good credit, a new house, a car, and a motorcycle. I worked twenty hours a week, had six weeks of vacation, my kids went to private school, and they had a nanny. Things had definitely changed.

When I opened the door, there stood Brienne looking so very different than the woman I ran into in the bookstore. She must have taken the extra time to get herself all done up. She looked good and I tried hard not to show my lust and just how taken I was.

"Brienne, hi. What are you doing here?"

"I decided to take a chance. I used your number to do a search and here I am. I needed to see you, to make things right. May I come in?"

"Um, sure."

With that, Brienne walked by me and into my home. The scent that drifted off of her was one that was familiar, exciting and soothing. She smelled so good, but smelling good was never our problem, so she would have to do more than smell good to make things right.

"Can I get you something to drink?"

"No, I'm good. I love the house. It's very nice."

"Thanks. I bought it a couple weeks ago when I got accepted into my practice."

"Congratulations. I see you still move fast. This place is on its way to being a masterpiece."

"So what can I do for you Brienne?"

"You sound so clinical."

"Well, it's not like I was expecting you or anything. You show up unannounced at my house and I never told you where I lived and we already spoke today, and I hung up on you. What more do you want, Brienne?"

I was trying to remain calm and stand firm. I had grown tired of the way things went between Brienne and I. I somehow always catered to her and let her take the easy way out. She very rarely apologized for the things she did, she just put it on her need to be free and not have to answer to anyone. I was in the wrong for stepping out like that. I was not about to apologize for expecting that the woman I was with would actually want to be with me and share her life, not hide me from everyone else that she knew. Things just got swept under the rug and just like all unresolved issues, it blew up in our faces and I walked out. For once, I wanted her to step up. If she could be so brazen and show up on my doorstep, she had better be ready. I had no more time in my life for games.

I was a young professional, looked good, had no emotional baggage and was looking forward to spending my summer decorating my new house, entertaining my friends and family, and blazing a trail down the highway on my new bike. Surely I would meet a woman who could love me and truly go there. Brienne was blocking traffic in my love life.

"So what's up?"

I knew why Nessa was making this so hard. What could I say? It's not like I didn't deserve it. I could never expect to just waltz back into her life as if it were a convenience store. I had hurt this woman more times than she or I cared to remember and here I was in her house, unannounced, getting ready to bare my soul. I had dreamt of this moment, dreaded it, feared it, and then finally got up the courage to face it. I went to therapy and did what I had to so I could be ready. This woman was the ONE and I was not going to let her go without a fight. She taught me how to fight for love and I was going to fight for her.

"I umm, I came over here to um...Vanessa, I love you with everything I have in me. I have known money, travel, education, endless opportunity, but I have never known love like what you have shown me and made me feel. I was a fool to let you leave and I am sorry that I hurt you so many times. I want to have a family with you. I want to come home to you and the kids every day, when I am happy, tired, upset, all of it. I need you, I want you and for the first time, I am not afraid to go there with you."

I was in shock. Never in a million years did I think Brienne would ever open her mouth and say anything like that. Before I could recover and respond, Brienne had gotten down on one knee and she held a jewelry box in her hand. When she opened it, I nearly fainted. Inside was the most beautiful ring I had ever seen.

"I looked at this ring and I saw you. It's beautiful as you are, it's set in platinum, one of the strongest metals, for you, one of the strongest women I know and this diamond is clear, perfectly cut and flawless, just like you. I know what I want Vanessa and it's you. It has always been you. Vanessa, would you do me the honor of being my partner for now and forever and wear this ring as a symbol of my love and commitment to you?

I stood there in shock thinking about my conversation earlier with Monica.

"Let it go? You are actually telling me to let it go? That woman would have to damn near walk on water to get back into my heart."

Did this woman just come into my house and ask me to marry her? Talk about walking on water. She had just parted the Red Sea.

"I don't know what to say."
"Say yes."

I looked at Brienne and for the first time in a long time I saw that familiar softness in her brown eyes. I loved this woman and because I knew her and our history, our journey, I knew how hard it was for her to do what she had just done, to take that chance and make herself so vulnerable to me. In the instant before I gave my answer, everything about my life with her, our love, my deepest feelings came over me in a flash. I loved this woman with all my heart and I wanted to spend my life with her.

"Yes, yes Brienne. I will marry you!"

With that, Brienne leapt up and put her arms around me and kissed me. She held me so tight and began to cry. She kissed me on the cheek and whispered, "I love you" in my ear. She released her grip and wiped away her tears to put the ring on my finger. It was a perfect fit and it had such brilliance. I felt like a princess. We hugged again and kissed for the first time in over a year.

"Where are the kids?"

"They are actually out with the nanny at the park. They should be back soon."

"Why don't you call the nanny and tell her to bring them home or we can go get them. I want to see my girls. I have missed them so much. We are going to be a family and I am so excited! We have so much to talk about, catch up on…. I love you Nessa. For the first time in my life, I feel whole. Thank you for loving me the way that you do."

I could not believe it. We got in the car and met the kids at the park. They were so excited to see Brienne and even more excited when we all went out together. We took things slowly, adjusting to the new changes in each other and even going to counseling. So much had changed, but our love for each other remained the same and grew stronger.

For once, I was able to take care of Brienne. Not that she needed it, but it was nice to pay all the bills, take her places, pay for vacations and lavish her with presents. She had calmed down so much and become much more open with herself with me than she had ever been. We eventually settled on a date for our wedding and she insisted on buying half of the house when she moved in. She said it was a reflection of her commitment. She even had papers drawn up to adopt the kids. Granted, they knew who their father was, but he really wasn't a contributing factor in their lives. I have never been happier.

My work schedule allowed me to be at home more and things are wonderful. Just recently, I took the family on a much needed vacation to the islands where we all got to run and play in the sun.

Brienne and I were married in front of our family and friends in a beautiful beachfront ceremony on June 4th. Just as the sun was setting, I walked up the aisle with Shania Twain crooning in the background, "Looks like we made it…" Brienne is still the one I love and the one I run to. My love, my best friend…Always.

Tanisha McMillan

<u>Chapter Ten</u>

B-A-B-Y-M-A-M-A
This goes out to all my baby mamas
I got love for all my baby mamas
-Fantasia, Baby Mama

This chapter is for all my women out there who are single mothers, holding it down, lesbian and straight, who just want someone in their lives, who are about something and willing to step up and be a parent. Not from the first date, but after a while and things get serious. If you aren't sure about being a parent or taking on some sort of parental role, stay away from a woman who has kids! I am writing this for all the times I ever argued with my girlfriend about being a parent, had to doubt myself and feel that the only way I was to ever have a family again was to deny myself and be with a man, and for the way the lesbians I know feel about kids. They love them as long as they are going home with someone else and if their girlfriends have kids, they are exactly that, HER kids.

It has taken a lot for me to realize that no matter what, it would always be just me when it came to the struggles of my life. Of course no one wants to believe such a thing, but I am learning that it is true. In the relationship that I sought to mend over and over again, it always seemed to be her needs over mine. I thought my needs were those of the relationship. I was more "we" than I was "I". Maybe that was my flaw. I stopped loving so hard and even changed my criteria for dating because of my experiences with her. I want the whole package because I am the whole package. If I am dating a woman with kids, I understand and accept that her kids will become a part of my life and I am ready to accept that responsibility. It only seems logical. My fear is that I will never come across a woman who will want to be there, share my parenting experience and grow old. Why is it so much harder for lesbians to become step-moms? Real men step up and take care of and raise another man's kids as if they were their own. So what's up with the women? Or are we so wrapped up in trying to live up to what we think a gay life is that we don't want to be tied down to kids, especially if they aren't ours?

I am a mom first, then a lesbian woman. In my world, it's a package deal if you want to get serious. You can't have me like that and exclude my kids. I want to take a moment to thank Fantasia Barrino for making the song "Baby Mama". It is reflective of the plight of many single mothers, including myself. I remember feeling a sense of pride when she won American Idol. I am sure now that she is in the spotlight a little bit, her life as a baby mama has gotten so much better. My hat is off to you Fantasia! It is a struggle from day one raising kids on your own and the last thing you need is someone half stepping into your life.

My experiences have taught me to be weary. As a single mother, I have no time to waste on grown folk's drama when I know I will need that energy for my kids. When you are a parent, all the drama should come from the kids. If it is coming from your lover/significant other/partner, you might want to check that.

Being a baby mama is something I never wanted to be. I wanted no part of being a statistic for the bureaucrats in Washington to scrutinize. I got married and there was definitely a distinction between being a baby's mama and a wife. In the end however, the result is still the same. I am a single parent. As a lesbian single parent, my experiences have taught me a great many things and I am getting to see a different part of the world and just how heterosexist it really is. Having young children in school really amplifies this. School events are focused on two parent homes that include a mommy and a daddy. Not all children have that. Some only have a mommy, some a daddy or two mommies or two daddies.

In everyday life, no one stops to think about those of us who don't fit into the nice categories of life. Luckily for me, my kids have not experienced any backlash or mistreatment because their mom is gay. Most of my kids' friends think I am a cool mom. I might not resemble their moms in the fact that I love my short hair, I can fix my own car, I love my Timberland boots and I ride a motorcycle, but I love my kids and that shows.

Chapter Eleven

I've been working the grave shift
And I ain't made shit
Sometimes I wish I could
Find me a spaceship and fly
-Kanye West,

A t the end of all this bullshit, I find myself reflecting on the path that I have been walking. It has been an interesting road from day to day. I have learned so much about myself and about the people around me and I have made some great friends along the way. I have discovered love, been hurt and found love again. Relationships require work. I don't think there is anyway around that. If you are not working just as hard at your relationship as you are at your job, your relationship is probably not going to be successful.

I used to think that my same sex relationships would be so much easier than any heterosexual one. I have since learned that its definitely not the case. Taking two people and blending their lives together takes a tremendous amount of work.

Aside from that, fixing yourself takes work. Here I am, still trying to find my niche. I have no idea what I want to be or what I am going to use my college degree for. Sometimes I find myself wondering just what I can do in this world where I can enjoy what I do and actually get paid for it. I am not going to lie. I want to be paid well even if it is something that I enjoy. Pure enjoyment does not pay the bills and I am well past the point in my life of delinquent notices.

I started writing this book for so many reasons and many of those reasons are different now. In the beginning it was about healing and moving on with my life and now it is about goals, dreams and possibilities. Maybe this writing thing is my calling. It is the one thing I have always been able to do and never paid much attention to. We never can see what is right in front of our faces. It took me a long time to accept that. Just because something came natural to me did not mean that it was any less satisfying or fulfilling. I had lots of questions as I got more into this process of writing. Will people actually respond to what I have written? Will it make people stop and think about the world in a different light? I certainly hope so. I wanted people to be able to laugh, cry, come to terms with certain situations in their lives, stop hurting over a lost relationship or just stop to think. Maybe take a moment to mend a broken relationship whether it is with a friend, relative or lost lover. These words here are about so much more than my lesbian experience. These words reflect a life lived, mistakes made, and obstacles overcome. My characters are reflections of people who have come into my life and had an impact on the person I have become. There were many steps that had to be taken for these words to grace these pages, but the point is, I took those steps, one at a time. I am learning to be grateful for the gift I have been given, the gift of writing. It has allowed me to enter into people's lives, their hearts and their minds and touch their spirits. There is no better gift than that and that is no bullshit!

<u>*ORDERING INFORMATION*</u>

To order extra copies of *Lesbian Bullshyt*, visit

www.obpublishing.com

Opal Book Publishing

5911 FISHER ROAD, SUITE 13
TEMPLE HILLS, MARYLAND 20748
obpublishing.info@gmail.com

Tanisha McMillan

www.ingramcontent.com/pod-product-compliance
Lightning Source LLC
Chambersburg PA
CBHW051925240626
47153CB00004B/1378